NETMINDER

CODENAME: WINGER #4

JEFF ADAMS

NETMINDER

CODENAME: WINGER #4

JEFF ADAMS

ONE

"WERE WE THAT AWKWARD AS FRESHMEN?" I asked Mitch as we drove toward my house. While I usually biked home, after the long practice, I took Mitch up on the offer of a ride. Coach had worked the team extra hard in an effort to get the newbies into the right flow. "I don't remember being that slow or having Coach repeat himself so much."

"We were quick to catch on to the drills, but we didn't move very fast. It was a few games into the season before he actually put us in."

When practice had started two weeks ago, the returning team members reelected Mitch captain. He deserved the recognition for his sportsmanship, leadership, and stellar gameplay.

I was proud to see my best friend retain the title he deserved.

"Maybe I just want to remember the good stuff." I shot a grin his direction, which he must've seen from the corner of his eye since he smiled too. "Why did Coach pick players who can't follow instructions, though? Makes you wonder who tried out if these were the best choices."

"They'll catch on," Mitch said. "We're the seniors, so it's on us to set a good example so they'll improve like we did. And so they'll do it when it's their turn in four years."

We did have great seniors on the team when we were freshmen. Of course Mitch wanted to be the same for these guys. "I'm sure we'll do you proud."

"Please let me talk to Coach about making you the alternate? Alternate Captain Theo Reese has a great ring to it."

Mitch had pursued this relentlessly for days, even during our August hockey camp.

Camp had distracted me from what happened in New York earlier in the summer. Mitch and I had one conversation about it before the trip. After that I'd done my best to forget Eddie's betrayal, but I'd still lost it a few times. Mitch helped me dry my eyes and put myself back together. Thankfully he didn't push me to talk since I couldn't give more details than the flimsy cover story.

Weeks later I knew nothing about the TOS investigation into the Cochranes and the double-cross Eddie had pulled. It was outside my clearance, even though it had happened to me. If Mom and Dad knew anything—and they might not—they justifiably kept me in the dark. Meanwhile, the mess created by what Eddie did hit a new level of drama once I returned to school.

Eddie was a constant topic of discussion—both to my face and behind my back. Eddie had been responsible for most of my social media content because he'd tag me a lot. With his Facebook profile deleted and him gone from school, everyone wanted to know what was up.

I'd deliberately posted nothing. The rumor mill kicked in while Mitch and I were at camp, though, because he tagged me in camp pictures. The story became that I'd ditched Eddie to go with Mitch. Iris, Mitch's girlfriend, vigorously told commenters not to be stupid.

Iris was awesome that way. She also stayed away from the topic of where Eddie had gone.

The swim team questioned me relentlessly. Eddie was one of the stars, and they didn't appreciate my silence.

Everyone expected I'd have a story to tell.

Uncomfortable didn't begin to cover how I felt. I became more socially awkward than I could remember ever being because so many people wanted to talk about *the* thing I didn't. I had no idea how much the school paid attention to our relationship.

Mitch stole glances at me. "You better tell me you're thinking about taking alternate. It's high time the team had one."

"Do you really think I'm a good choice when I'm already crazy busy?" I said, hoping to cover my Eddie spiral.

My watch pulsed with a notification, and I glanced at it. John went into my room.

Strange.

I couldn't remember a time that he'd entered my room without me at home. My security system's biometric doorknob would admit only four people—me, my parents, and John. What would he need in there?

I wasn't on a mission currently, focusing instead on upgrades to the ways agent phones and TOS apps interacted with Siri for voice commands. It was an easy way to get back into the swing of TOS after camp.

Mitch kept looking over, and I recognized the look. He was about to say something he thought I didn't want to hear. "Have you considered that you might work too much?" He capped the question with a smile.

"Yeah," I said with a groan attached. "Camp was epic and exactly the reset I needed. So, yeah, it's possible."

"Could I convince you to be alternate just by reminding you that I'm your captain?" Mitch pulled into the driveway alongside John's car. He put the car in park and gave me a stern look.

John and I had held down the home front for a week. Mom went to Portland to train agents on how to handle the effects of being deep undercover. Dad, meanwhile, continued on a mission somewhere in Europe. In an odd way it comforted me to know they were good going away at the same time since they'd watched over my emotional health so much, even after camp. It showed we'd all started to move past the insanity of what had gone down before camp.

"Wouldn't it be an abuse of power?" It was an honor that he'd asked, but I didn't want to let him down if I had to put my attention elsewhere.

"All I'm doing is appealing to you as my friend, my teammate…. And someone who falls under my authority."

He tried to hold a serious face and failed, which ultimately cracked us both up.

"You need to work on that if you're going to try and influence people with that look." I smirked at him as I grabbed my pack and opened the door. "I'll see you in the morning. Thanks for the ride. Later, man."

We traded a fist bump before I closed the door. The hatch lifted as I came around to the back to unload my bike.

After gently pushing on the hatch so it'd close, I moved out of the way, so he could pull out. We traded a last wave as he passed.

I triggered the garage door with my phone.

Something felt off.

I racked the bike and gave it the usual end of day once-over but couldn't shake the odd feeling.

Nothing was out of place. Both cars were gone, and the stuff we stored—Christmas decorations, yard work tools, and random things in bins—looked undisturbed.

If I were Peter Parker, I'd say that my Spidey-sense was tingling.

My imagination must've gone off the rails. It had to be an overreaction to the notification about John going into my room.

In the kitchen the feeling intensified.

"John?" I called out as I grabbed a water from the fridge.

No response.

The office door stood open. Anxiety spread, tightening my chest.

The room was empty, though there was a smell I couldn't place.

John's laptop stood open on his desk and his screensaver with the moving clock ran.

A photo on Dad's desk lay facedown. Weird. Maybe John had bumped the desk. I went to put it back in place.

I dropped the picture frame when I caught sight of his legs behind the desk. They were askew, one lying over the other.

"John!"

Had he collapsed?

I stopped short as I took in all of him. A pool of blood spread across his shirt.

That was the smell. I gagged, trying to keep from throwing up.

Shit.

His right hand was gone, blood spilled from his wrist. A cleaver lay next to him.

Jesus.

I stumbled backward, feet not working right.

Someone cut off his hand. He hadn't gone into my room at all....

The office spun, and I grabbed Dad's chair to steady myself. I couldn't pass out.

Was he dead?

I dropped my backpack and knelt next to him.

I should call.... Call who?

John was the one I called when shit went down, and my parents weren't home. We weren't supposed to call 911 for agents, but this....

I breathed through my mouth to minimize the smell.

The pulse in his uninjured wrist was barely there. His chest showed a very slight rise and fall.

"John!"

I flinched at the volume. There could still be people in the house. People in my room.

"John?" I was quieter and shook him gently.

First aid training didn't cover this. Maybe I could stop the bleeding. I needed something to tie off the arm. I unbuckled his belt, but it wouldn't slide out.

"Theo." He struggled to speak. His eyes barely fluttered open. "Run."

"But...."

"Run." His voice became crystal clear. "Now."

His hand clamped on my arm. I wanted to scream... or cry... or both.

"Go!" His eyes focused intensely on me for a couple of seconds and then shut.

His hand dropped.

Training kicked in. We had protocols for this.

When I was thirteen, Mom and Dad decided we

needed a plan "just in case." I never imagined we'd use it, not even after Eddie's betrayal.

I'd call 911 and TOS after I was gone. I hoped John could be saved.

John's instructions couldn't be ignored.

I grabbed my pack and ran upstairs, slowing when I saw my open door.

John's hand was on the floor.

Fuck.

I listened. No sound came from the room. I approached slowly, quietly, ready to defend myself.

Inside all the electronics were gone, including the stuff that was just for show. How'd they get it out without looking like a robbery?

I pulled my phone and it shook. I hadn't realized how I quaked.

It took longer than it should, but I sent the signal to fry the computers. I spared the phone and the laptop in my backpack, for now.

Frantically I threw stuff out of the closet—boxes of textbooks, my stash of Red Wings trading cards, spare computer parts, and other things I didn't use much. At least they hadn't been in here.

I removed a couple of the floor boards to reach my go stash—an unregistered phone, alternate ID, two thousand dollars cash, and some debit cards. I stuffed it all in one of the hidden compartments of my backpack.

The desk was a disaster with cables yanked from computers. Papers and knickknacks scattered across the surface and onto the floor. Drawers were pulled out too, and the contents were shuffled. They'd left behind what I wanted, though—the latest contact lens prototype. They were stored in a common lens case and that must've saved them.

My phone and watch beeped. The signal had gone out. Once any of my computers came online, they'd be toast. Between that and the security I had in place on the devices, no one should get anything sensitive.

The shakes intensified—adrenaline, shock, both. I almost dropped the phone.

I took a deep breath.

And another.

My voice had to be steady.

On the TOS phone, I placed an unsecured call to Mom.

She picked up after two rings. "Theo, what a nice surprise. You caught me getting some coffee between sessions. How was your day?"

"It was good." Thank God I had practice trying to sound calm when I was anything but. "We had a grueling practice trying to whip the freshmen into shape. And Mitch is still trying to convince me to be alternate."

"I think you'd be good at that. But I won't say more. I'll leave the persuading to him." She was proud he asked me, and she'd done some subtle campaigning for it. All part of me being a teenager as much as possible.

I took an extra deep breath.

"Yeah, he's really laying it on. Anyway, I wanted to let you know I'm going to Roger's house to work on a project."

Roger's house was the code we'd set up in case I was in danger and going into hiding.

"Okay. Tell Roger's mom I said hello." Another pause. No doubt she had the same struggle I did—what to say given the circumstances. "My break's wrapping up, so I need to get back. And you should go before it gets too dark." Always a mom.

"Thanks, Mom. I love you."

"Love you too, Theo." I heard the concern, the slightest fault in her voice. I doubted anyone who might be listening would register it. "See you in a few days."

We disconnected. I looked at the screen for just a moment before I pocketed the phone.

I had to go.

TWO

I LOOKED around the room and fought the urge to sit on the floor and freak out. I didn't know when I'd get back here.

And how do I leave John?

He wouldn't leave me. He'd protect me.

Which he was doing.

He told me to go.

At the window I checked the surroundings. The second-floor vantage point proved useful.

The windows of our house had a slight tint. The high-tech glass kept people from looking in even if they were right up against the glass. It didn't appear as totally dark from the street, and at night, lights from the rooms shined out.

Traffic on the street appeared normal with people coming home from work. However, there were two cars on the street parked almost perfectly equidistant from our house. Were those there when Mitch dropped me off? From this distance it was difficult to tell if anyone was inside.

Two people walked on the sidewalk, approaching from the southwest—the most direct route in and out of the neighborhood. The woman stole a glance at the parked car as she passed.

I didn't recognize either of them. I'd lived in this house all of my life. Not only did I know everybody on the street, but I knew most of the neighborhood because of the block parties that happened a few times a year. Plus, for safety, we knew quite a bit about who lived around us.

These people, those cars, they could be part of another attack. Did they know I was here?

John was right—I had to get out.

I grabbed the pack off the floor and scrambled down the stairs as fast as I could. Going out the front door would be stupid. I stopped there, though, and engaged the three locks. From the garage, I'd arm the security system. If they came back, it'd go off and at least alert the cops.

I ran through the house, back the way I'd come. In the garage I unracked the bike and got ready to go into the backyard.

The alarm wouldn't set. I entered the codes again but instead of a confirmation that it would arm in ten seconds nothing happened.

What the hell?

I tried again, but nothing.

They'd done something. No time to figure it out.

Backpack across my shoulders, I burst out the back door and sprinted across the yard to the fence line, rolling the bike next to me.

I heaved the bike over the fence, which was slightly taller than I was. Regret shot through me at having done that to my expensive, fine-tuned machine. There was no choice, though.

Hockey conditioning came in handy as I pulled myself

up the wood planks that had no footholds. I dropped next to the bike, which had landed in a pile of brush.

Looking around, memories rushed back. When we were kids, Mitch and I, along with other friends, would play hide and seek, laser tag and Indiana Jones in these woods. There were plenty of paths and, even though I hadn't been back here in years, the routes were as clear as ever.

I pulled the phone and called 911.

A woman answered with authority, "911. What's your emergency?"

"I need an ambulance at 1321 Remington Way." My voice cracked and quivered. "My uncle. He's hurt." A whimper escaped. "Please hurry."

"What's his injury?"

"Someone... he's been... he's bleeding."

Should I say he's shot? Or missing a hand? Keeping details to just enough to get them here seemed enough.

"I'm sending an ambulance and police. Where's he bleeding from?"

"He's...." I could barely talk anymore.

"Take a deep breath and try to calm down. Help is on the way. We can stay on the phone until...." Her voice shifted into a calmer tone that was more than I could handle.

I gulped air. "He's been shot and... and... I just got home."

"Where's the gun now?"

I hung up. She couldn't help me. I had to pull myself together and get going. John would be okay. He had to be.

He told me to go. He knew I'd follow his order.

What if that was wrong?

I couldn't change it now. I had to go before anyone came.

I righted the bike, gave it a quick check, and got on as sirens sounded in the distance.

As I rode I kept my eyes on the trail, trying to dodge potholes, sticks, rocks, and debris that could damage the bike. The repair kit I had with me wasn't going to be useful if I destroyed the tires. This was a road bike, not a BMX.

I wouldn't be in the woods long. If I recalled right, the path I chose would bring me out as far from the house as possible.

It wasn't long before I had to get off the bike as the terrain got tougher.

Before I went farther, I pulled out my TOS phone. Checking in with Lorenzo was required. I suspected Mom had already alerted him, but he needed to know my status and check-in plan.

The phone wouldn't go into secure mode because it couldn't lock on to the signal.

The TOS secure network was more robust and widespread than cell networks. Being out of range was nearly impossible.

Running a few diagnostics, the phone kept reporting no signal. There was no malfunction indicated, though.

TOS wouldn't cut me off. If anything, they'd be trying to contact me. Lorenzo would've been automatically notified I'd requested the computers be destroyed.

In seven years I'd never seen an outage. The network had many fail-safes and redundancies.

I'd have to sort it out later. I might've stood still too long already.

The bike's light weight made it easy to carry but climbing over some of the brush wasn't easy. Emerging in a neighborhood adjacent to ours, I paused to dig out the unregistered phone from my pack. It had enough charge to power up, but it needed to be plugged in as soon as I could stop.

Where should I go? Going south would lead back to MIT, and that was too obvious. I opened Google Maps. Since the phone and apps weren't registered, any data couldn't be traced to me, making this the safest way possible to research places to go.

North, toward Tufts University could work. There'd be plenty of Wi-Fi. While I couldn't access any of the buildings—I wouldn't want to flash my MIT ID—there'd be places to settle for a few minutes to make a plan. It also wouldn't take too long to get there.

Usually riding in traffic didn't bother me, but this trip made me crazy because every car could be a threat. Plus I didn't have my lights attached, and the safety issues caused additional anxiety. While the lights were in my pack, I didn't want to take the time to connect them. I'd deal with that later. At least the streets were well lit.

At the edge of the Tufts campus, I used the phone to look for a coffee shop.

Four blocks away was a Starbucks.

As I locked the bike against a light pole in front of the café's window, I noted the crowd inside and hoped it meant I'd easily blend in. I quickly got a chicken pesto sandwich along with a venti mocha—infusing chocolate into coffee was the only way I liked it. At the register I caught myself just before I used Apple Pay. Almost a rookie mistake using something so easily traced.

I stuffed the phone back into my pocket and pulled out my wallet. Luckily I had a ten. Next time I was alone, I'd move some of the cash to allow easy access.

At a communal table, I wedged in between a hipster and a guy who murmured into his earbud mic. Across the table sat two women, most likely in college, having an animated conversation, and a sullen guy staring into his iced drink. Unwrapping the sandwich, I casually looked around and didn't see anything out of place. It was difficult not to keep watching, but I didn't want to look suspicious.

With the TOS phone I got on Wi-Fi and took care to make sure it couldn't be traced.

The phone held no clues about what happened to the TOS network. Regular cellular service had no disruption. There were plenty of Wi-Fi signals between Starbucks, personal hotspots, and other businesses nearby. On the secure part of the phone, though, there was no signal and no reason for there not to be either. All the apps were still there. If someone at TOS had taken out my phone in the way I had done to my stolen electronics, the phone would've been completely dead.

Dammit.

With no TOS network, my computers wouldn't get destroyed. Maybe they got the signal before the system went down.

I gulped down the sandwich. This place would only be open for about ninety minutes before it's nine o'clock closing, so I couldn't waste time coming up with a plan.

What did I need to do?

In the missions I'd been on so far, even if I was temporarily cut off from TOS, I knew they were out there, and they'd establish contact, rescue me, whatever.

But now....

Even my parents didn't know how to find me. They only knew that something had gone wrong.

I wanted to call Mom or Dad. The teenager wanted what the agent couldn't allow. I would only call them when

I thought I had the situation under control. I wouldn't risk breaking the protocol we set up.

The plan, however, had never considered that TOS might be under attack.

There was something to try, though. An outside chance.

I pulled the unregistered phone from my pack along with the charger cord since it needed juice. From the TOS phone, I got Lorenzo's personal number. We were friends outside of work often playing video games together.

I keyed in the number, saved it, and hit dial.

"Hey, you've reached Lorenzo. Busy as usual. Tell me what's up after the beep."

Dammit.

Straight to voicemail like the phone was off rather than ignoring a number he didn't recognize.

There was another way to hopefully get his attention.

I sent a text: *It's Red Turingdor. Some weird shit's going down in Azeroth. Could really use the help of Tron the Great. Hit me up.*

Our Minecraft character names should get his attention, but for anyone intercepting his texts it shouldn't obviously lead back to me. A shot in the dark but worth it.

No one tells you how to work when all the support is gone or when you've left someone behind. What if I'd made the wrong choice not doing more for John? Maybe I should've stood my ground at the house and had TOS dispatch help. Or... I didn't know.

THREE

Where could I hole up for the night?

The farther away from home, the better. There were so many ways to be tracked with cameras—traffic, ATM, other businesses with street surveillance not to mention the tracker chip in my neck. Starbucks had at least two visible cameras—provided neither was fake. Staying invisible was difficult at best.

Riding with the helmet gave me some cover but not a lot.

Back to Maps, I looked for cheap hotels that weren't more than an hour's ride away. Cheap was key. While I had the stash of cash and cards, there was no way to know how long it needed to last.

I found a place where rooms cost just over a hundred dollars and that was less than five miles away.

Lightning flashed outside the window and a rolling crack of thunder followed in short order.

Great.

I didn't mind riding in the rain. Sometimes it relaxed me. A thunderstorm was another matter.

It was time to hit the road, before the storm arrived.

Almost out the door, I stopped and went back to get a couple more cold sandwiches and bottles of water, so I'd have another meal on hand.

Hopefully, the hotel would have a room. While I could've booked online, I didn't want to leave any traces.

Drizzle fell. Lightning vividly arched across the sky. Thunder gave a low, ominous rumble—it was the low bass of an action movie amplified in extreme surround sound.

I couldn't remember what I'd learned in grade school about how to count from the lightening flash to the thunder clap to figure out how far the storm was.

I didn't pause to Google that. I got the lights mounted and took off.

Once at the hotel, my priority would be to attempt to resurrect the TOS network and get help. Tracking down who'd invaded the house was a close second.

I'd solved a lot of problems, but people invading the house, doing what they did to John, no TOS network—it all seemed much bigger than my abilities to fix.

The weather went to hell after I'd been on the road for a couple of minutes. A downpour soaked me in a matter of seconds. At least the backpack was waterproof. If I was lucky, the hotel had a laundry room.

Riding in the rain sucks when you don't know the terrain. The GPS provided instructions in my earbuds, but without the phone mounted on the handlebars, I couldn't see the preview of the road's curves.

It took longer than expected to get to the hotel. At least there weren't any jerks on the road. Most drivers gave me space, didn't try to crowd, and even when the road narrowed, they went around without a honk. It didn't seem like anyone followed me, but I couldn't be completely sure.

The hotel looked decent. Surprisingly, it had a bike rack near the front door, which was even under an overhang. Now I wouldn't have to talk them into allowing me to bring the bike to the room, so it didn't get further soaked.

I took off the helmet and hung it off the handlebars. Looking around, I tried to take in everything as I ran my hand through my hair to dry it out as best I could. I pulled the lock from my pack and secured the bike.

Putting on my best confident look, I slung the pack over one shoulder, took my helmet in hand, and went for the door. The lobby was warm and made me shudder. I hadn't realized how cold I'd become.

"Good evening, how can I—" The woman at the front desk stopped short as she looked up and saw my disheveled state. "Goodness. You got caught out in it. How can I help you? Checking in?"

She looked unsure, but at least she wasn't telling me to get out as I dripped on the tiled floor. "I hope you've got a room. I was out cycling, trying to beat the storm and failed."

I tried not to let my teeth chatter and sound like it was normal for someone to be on a bike on a night like this as if they were headed somewhere even farther away. It didn't help that I looked my age. Some of my classmates could easily pass as college age, but I looked like a high schooler. Usually I didn't care, but tonight I needed to sell being older.

"I have some rooms available, yes." She continued to sound unsure. "I'm sorry, but I have to ask, are you over eighteen? I can't give a room to a minor."

I smiled, wanting it to look like I got this all the time. "Oh, yes, of course. Let me get you my ID and credit card."

Dropping my backpack to the floor so it would only add water to the existing puddle, I retrieved the wallet with my fake driver's license and the cards. The Massachusetts driver's license identified me as Jason Robert Karr, age eighteen, along with a MasterCard that would get me through this transaction. Before I stood I slipped my regular wallet into the pack since I didn't know when I'd be Theo Reese again.

I handed over the cards.

She studied them and then smiled apologetically as if sorry for doubting. "Do you have any room preferences, Mr. Karr?"

"Anything with a hot shower is fine."

She nodded and clicked away on her keyboard. "Checking out in the morning?"

I hadn't considered that. If I stayed here, I'd have a base of operations and Wi-Fi. If I wanted to get farther from Boston, I should arrange a new ID. Renting a car was tough if you were under twenty-five. I had to figure that out tonight.

"Two days, please."

She studied her screen. "We can accommodate that." She typed more, talking as she went. "Are you on a bike trip or something? I saw you ride up." She gestured at the doors where my bike was visible.

"Yeah." I wasn't going to debate the cover she created for me. "It's been great. Until tonight."

She smiled and nodded as she ran the card key over the device that coded it for my room.

"You're all set. Second floor, room two twenty-five. Elevators are just down the hall on your right. We have a continental breakfast served from six to nine. If you need anything tonight, there are vending machines on each floor and there are a couple of places that deliver as well. Can I do anything else for you?"

"Is there a laundry room? It'd be great to dry these things out." I gestured at my wet clothes.

"Oh yes, of course. On the third floor in the corner." She pointed. "If you've got some cash, I'll give you some quarters."

I dug five dollars out of my wallet and traded it.

"Thank you. I wouldn't have thought of that right off." She smiled again. I guess somehow I'd charmed her. "Thanks so much for your help."

"My pleasure, Mr. Karr. If you need anything else this evening, you can dial zero and I'll see what we can do."

My sneakers squeaked and made squishing sounds as I went to the elevators. I wasn't going to be able to dry the shoes quickly. If there was a hair dryer in the room maybe I could use that. Cold, wet shoes would suck tomorrow.

The room was basic. Given all the travel hockey I'd played, this was a familiar setting. In the bathroom, I set the pack down and stripped before pulling dry clothes out. At least I could be dry.

Dressed in jeans and a Red Wings sweatshirt, I got everything out of the pack. I struggled to focus on the task. Images of John filled my mind. I couldn't shake them—a nightmare while wide awake.

I thought about my parents too. They'd bought me the pack I used because it allowed things like my TOS comms, the contact lenses and the stash of cash I now carried to be tucked into secret areas. Were Mom and Dad okay? If someone got into the house had they been found too?

I sighed.

The waterproof pack would dry fast, so I hung it on one of the hooks behind the bathroom door.

The reflection in the mirror caught me off guard. Dad and I were similar in appearance—no mistaking we were related. Momentarily it felt like he looked back at me. I heaved a giant sob and stepped back a couple of paces only to run into the tub. I ended up sitting down for a moment on the tub's edge before sliding down to the floor.

I sat in stunned silence for a moment before the sobs came hard and fast.

The sound echoed around the small bathroom—so much so it wouldn't have surprised me if someone reported the noise. It wouldn't stop.

John was.... I didn't know.

I didn't have Mom and Dad.

Winger lost out to Theo—and not just Theo but kid Theo who really wanted a hug from his parents and hear that everything was going to be okay. Somehow, though, I had to be an agent and do... something.

A shudder started in the middle of my chest and spread. It was small, but it refused to stop.

This wasn't the time to freak out.

Shudders became quakes, and I struggled to be quiet. I couldn't draw attention to myself.

Closing my eyes, I tried to use the relaxation exercises Shields, my TOS counselor, had taught me.

Deep breath slowly in. Hold for a count of three. Exhale slowly.

And repeat.

No amount of repeating held back my tears.

FOUR

I'D SPENT the time my clothes dried looking for the TOS network. I couldn't get to any network or application login screen and even the IP addresses of servers I knew didn't ping back. It could all be turned off, but that didn't seem possible. It could be hijacked in some way—cloaked behind a new firewall or moved to new addresses. But why?

Not only did the network seem fried, but I couldn't execute any of the emergency protocols. While texting Lorenzo didn't appear on the list of things to do in an emergency, trying to reach anyone on official channels—both on and off the secure network—failed with just silence. Even the designated *last-chance* phone number simply rang. Theoretically that last-chance number should always be answered because it was a standard landline number in a secure, always manned location. I didn't know where it was, but I envisioned something like a military bunker.

Once I'd exhausted attempts to find the network, I decided to do something I'd put off. There might be some clues on the security footage from the house.

I accessed the videos from our home cloud, which

thankfully worked normally. Changing my password was the first order of business in case my computers landed in the wrong hands while fully operational.

I started from about twenty minutes before I got home. I chose feeds for the front door, the door coming in from the garage, the patio, in and outside of Mom and Dad's office, and in and outside of my room.

John was at his desk, and outside two men and a woman dressed in casual business attire—khakis and polo shirts—came down the sidewalk. They'd parked outside of the camera's range. As they turned up our walk, the woman came to the door, but the other two peeled away, going to either side of the porch and out of camera range.

John didn't check the cameras before he went to the door.

I paused and took a breath. While I knew the final outcome, I couldn't stop the tension seizing me.

I finally clicked Play.

John opened the door and appeared to have a regular conversation until the woman stepped forward. She pulled something from her pocket that I couldn't see. John stepped back, and the two others charged inside quickly and closed the door. They moved from the front hall, and for a few painfully long seconds, they were off-screen. When they came back, John walked in front of them, hands up, toward his desk. John and the woman talked.

Why had I never added mics to these cameras?

My heart raced.

John looked calm while one of the men got agitated and appeared to yell. More words. Suddenly the upset man pulled a gun from his waistband and fired. John's hand went to his chest, and he crumpled to the floor. The trio went crazy, screaming at each other. They quickly left the office.

John appeared to struggle, but I couldn't see anything other than his legs.

It didn't take long for them to show up outside my door. There's no way John told them anything about me or what was in the room. These guys already knew the layout of the house.

They tried the door, but it didn't open.

Attempting to break down the reinforced door also failed. There were no sensors in place to detect slamming into the door, but had it been forced open, alarms would've gone off.

The woman studied the door, the frame, and the wall surrounding it. She focused on the doorknob, crouching down to examine it. To a casual observer the doorknob looked like any other, but if you got close enough, you'd see the biometric sensors.

The group soon retreated back toward the stairs.

I fast-forwarded over the gruesome parts. The woman watched as the men did the dirty work. I couldn't take my eyes off the cleaver cutting through the air.

Once they had the hand, they hustled back upstairs, opened the door, and immediately went to my desk. They yanked out cables and took all of the CPUs. They looked through the desk, drawers, the dresser, and even a quick look in the closet but didn't take anything else.

A gray SUV pulled into the driveway, and another man and woman got out. Inside the house, the man went upstairs while the woman went toward the kitchen. She went into the pantry. Thirty seconds later, while the guys carried the equipment out, the video went dark.

She'd done something to the security system. No wonder I couldn't arm it when I left.

They'd been in the house for six minutes and thirteen seconds before the video cut.

Mitch and I missed them by less than five.

My God.

I gently closed the laptop, quelling my desire to slam it shut.

If we'd been any faster—left practice without Mitch calling Iris about their date or not catching so many red lights—he would've ended up in the middle of it.

And John.

Was he okay? Did they save him? *Could* they save him?

Searching for information on whether it was possible to survive having your hand cut off provided the smallest hope. If the cut happened in exactly the right way and proper medical attention could be administered, the person could be saved.

There'd been a lot of blood—was it too much?

Had I called in time?

"Please, God," I whispered. "You don't hear from me much. But if there's anything you can do for John... please...." Tears fell, but I didn't lose control like I had earlier. "Make him be okay. And please look out for everyone else too. If you're there, somewhere, you know how messed up things are."

FIVE

I JERKED awake because of the buzzing.

Light came from the TV, which I'd left on low volume. I didn't usually sleep with noise, but I'd tossed and turned for a half hour before I decided some noise might help distract my brain from grinding on all of the problems.

It only helped a little. I slept in short bursts and felt terrible as I attempted to force my tired eyes to focus as a dull throb pulsed across the back of my head.

The buzz went off again, and I recognized the pattern as Mitch's. A glance at my watch showed he was texting and that it was six thirty. He'd be on his way to pick me up—if he wasn't already there.

Crap.

I should've told him last night not to pick me up.

I propped myself against the headboard and grabbed my phone from the nightstand.

Are you all right? I just drove by your house and there's three black SUVs there and a scary-looking dude outside the front door. I'm around the corner if you want me to pick you up. Let me know.

Who was at the house? It sounded like more than the regular police. Was TOS looking for me? Had Mom sent them? Or was it whoever had been in the house yesterday?

I pulled my legs to my chest and held them to me while I dropped my head onto my knees. I didn't know what to do.

Another buzz from Mitch.

You're freaking me out. Text me back.

Shit.

What could I tell him, so he wouldn't worry?

Staring at the screen didn't help.

Unlocking the phone with my thumb, I stared at the messages. He'd know I'd seen them.

I typed: *Sorry. Should've texted. John's meeting some people for Mom and Dad. I left early. Catch you at school.*

I sent it and almost immediately the three dots appeared as he typed. In a few seconds the response arrived.

No worries. Just glad you're okay. Tell your parents they need less scary colleagues. Didn't expect to be freaked out first thing.

Mitch knew the basic cover for my parents with the FBI and Homeland Security jobs and that John worked with them.

Of course, this would only satisfy Mitch until he got to school and discovered I wasn't there. Eventually news about John would get out, unless somebody was already keeping that quiet. That had to be why so many people were at the house.

Maybe TOS had mobilized without the network. A quick look in the corner of the phone screen showed that the network icon wasn't present. Maybe I could find Lorenzo now or.... I still didn't know what the *or* could be. My parents, John, and Lorenzo were the only ones I had personal contact information for. I didn't even have Coach Daly's number for security reasons.

I rested my head against the headboard and considered my options.

I must've dozed off.

Vibrations on my wrist and the phone in my hand woke me up. Several messages from Mitch were on my watch. He must be in school because normally if he had that much to say he'd call.

Iris had sent messages too, as did others who didn't have a unique vibration pattern. The notification list filled up with texts from many friends and teammates.

I found the phone on the bed next to me and went to Mitch's:

Where the hell are you? There are clones of the dude that was at your front door at the school. People are looking for you. I told the one the principal made me talk to that I haven't seen you since I dropped you off last night. Which is true. But where are you? I won't tell them I just need to know you're okay.

I had no idea if someone was over Mitch's shoulder watching as he typed. It was better for him if I said nothing.

Three dots appeared.

Come on man. I know you just read that.

I turned the phone off.

Whether it was TOS or others, looking for me at school was not subtle. Someone was taking extraordinary efforts to get me.

But why? And were other TOS agents being tracked too?

Lying to Mitch rattled me to the core. Hopefully he'd understand if I got through this.

Without warning, a sob choked its way out. Clutching the phone, I wished I could control myself better.

What would Mom and Dad do if they were cut off? We didn't talk much about scenarios like this. When we'd set up the protocols for having to escape, we assumed that we'd be able to use TOS to reconnect, and that if we weren't talking directly, we'd be able to pass messages, get to a safe house, something.

I worked through Shield's calming techniques hoping they'd work better than they had last night. I had work to do. I'd hacked TOS security when I was eleven. I should be able to find a way out of this—either to fix the network or track down the people who broke it.

I sat up straight and wiped my sleeve over my face.

If someone had control of the network, I had to disable the tracker chip. I'd also have to assess the security of the rest of my electronics to make sure I stayed out of sight.

The TOS phone required modifications to knockout its tracking. Ditching the phone wasn't an option, though, because it had functions that didn't require the network, and I needed all the tools I could get.

I probably should've reviewed all of the security measures last night, but I'd kept looking for the network and trying the emergency protocols until I'd been too tired to go on. Given the crazy going on at home, this morning's priority revolved around becoming as invisible as possible.

SIX

As soon as my feet hit the floor from rolling out of bed, my stomach rumbled. I got the sandwich and water I'd bought last night from the fridge and nibbled on it while getting online.

I reviewed the security of the connection I'd set up last night. The IPs and geolocation were scrambled, so the computer should be solid. Without the TOS network, the secure phone would only be traceable on the regular cell network. But if someone else had control of the network, they could be tracking me even though they hadn't revealed themselves yet.

The phone was easy to disable—at least for me since I'd worked on its security. With the phone connected to the computer, I accessed the root systems and removed the code that handled the tracking.

The more difficult problem was the tracker chip. If I could access the network, I could likely hack the agent list to remove myself since I'd been part of the team that reworked the software after Blackbird had breached the system.

I had to get rid of the chip. I chomped on the sandwich while I considered how to do that.

It was behind my right ear. Running my hand over the skin, I easily found the small scar. It'd been removed and later replaced almost a year ago because of the Blackbird attack on the system. The surgical procedure was quick and painless with a local anesthesia.

Getting it out on my own would be the opposite.

The tool kit in my pack had a small pocket knife, along with a couple of screwdrivers, lockpicks, scissors, and first aid items like Band-Aids and alcohol wipes. Mom and Dad had given it to me after Denver, and it mirrored kits they traveled with. I'd augmented it with some tech items as well, like various chargers and connectors.

No one anticipated I'd attempt minor surgery with what I had.

I took the tool kit and went into the bathroom, very unsure of my plan. A not-so-subtle voice in my head said in no uncertain terms that I was crazy for trying this.

Grabbing one of the alcohol wipes, I tore it open, so I could clean the spot where I'd poke a hole in my neck. I used another to clean the knife.

This was gonna become number one on the suck list. I didn't like blood, and I was about to slice into my neck in an area I couldn't see, hoping to extract something not much bigger than a grain of rice.

Knife in my right hand, I intended to push the knife in and pop the chip out. I guided the knife with my left hand, awkwardly stretched behind my head.

My hands shook. The point of the knife poked my skin, but I couldn't bring myself to drive it in.

What the hell was I doing?

This was insanity. I couldn't get this out. One slip and

I'd be done for. Of course, if I'm caught, it could be just as bad.

There weren't enough deep breaths to calm me.

I pulled back and sat the knife on the countertop. I didn't want blood on my clothes, so I stripped out of the T-shirt I'd slept in and hung it on the doorknob.

From what I remembered from biology, most of the blood vessels that could bleed too fast and kill me were in the front of the neck. Bio wasn't my subject, so I could be wrong.

The doctor had used tweezers to remove it once. While I had a pair, I didn't think it'd be effective since I couldn't see. It'd be a blind game of Operation.

There had to be a better way.

The chip had microelectronics inside and the design was fairly simple since it only emitted a signal.

Jamming the signal could be done but doing that was enough outside my expertise that I couldn't guarantee doing it right.

Oh... oh! Maybe I could turn it off.

We'd developed a way for the TOS phones to emit an electromagnetic pulse of varying power. It could be very low and targeted or go big and even take out the phone itself. It shouldn't take much to knock out the chip.

I pulled my shirt back on and got the phone. I hadn't worked on this app, but I'd been trained on it and had even used it once.

I reviewed the settings. I wanted to choose the half-foot setting since I wanted enough power to ensure neutralization. As an extra precaution I decided to go outside and move away from the hotel in case something went wrong. I didn't want to be responsible for a widespread electrical problem.

I'd noticed when I'd arrived that the hotel had a field next to and behind it.

After leaving my watch and wallet in the room, I headed out. The only thing besides the phone that I took was the room key. In the field I went a dozen or so feet from the building, and I even left the key on a rock at a safe distance too.

I probably didn't need to take so many safety measures, but I had enough problems without creating more.

After unlocking the phone, I double checked the settings on the app and put it against my neck.

"Pulse," I said.

"Five," the phone's voice responded, "four, three, two, one. Pulse."

I felt the slightest twinge... at least I thought I did. Maybe I imagined it.

"Complete."

Or maybe the sensation came from the tracker's destruction. I'd have to hope this worked as planned.

SEVEN

Back in the room, I took an inventory of the tools I had. The phone still connected to my personal cloud, so I had access to the code snippets, scripts, and bots. I copied those to the phone in case I lost access. Looking at the apps, there were some I ignored because they wouldn't work without the secure network.

The contact lenses, however, had some functions powered solely from the phone that could come in handy. In fact these could verify the tracker was offline.

Before I crashed last night, I'd restored everything in the backpack in case I had to move quick. I fished out the lenses and went into the bathroom to put them in.

The lenses had been valuable a couple of times in New York this summer. In the months since then, we'd made improvements. Not only had the lens been modified to be more comfortable to wear for extended periods, but the night vision was much clearer. We'd also added infrared along with some other enhancements, including zoom and messaging functions. Getting text messages directly to the eye had major benefits. I hated sending them, though—I didn't get along well with the eye targeting keyboard. The team was working to refine it, however, so one day I hoped it would be better.

As soon as they made full contact with my cornea, they activated and read my biometric signature.

Whoa! Not only did the lens connect to my phone as it should, but it also connected to the TOS network. The square that displayed in the top left would've been yellow if it only found the phone. Green meant network connectivity. That might be my way in.

But first, I could use the lens to look at data streams. The development team built in the abilities to see electric currents, Wi-Fi signals, and data flows along fiber optic cables. They would also detect the signal the tracker put out, which was similar to Wi-Fi.

I accessed the menus via the eye tracking and activated all the data flows at once. Suddenly I saw the waves of signals coming off the phone, fiber optics in the walls and Wi-Fi emanating from the router in the hall. Using the shaving mirror bolted to the wall, I could see the back of my neck, and there was no signal coming from me.

Just to prove I could see signals through the mirrors, I slipped my phone into my back pocket, and I continued to see the signal waves.

Score! The tracker was offline.

A small speech bubble appeared in my vision. Had someone been testing the lenses yesterday? There were only three pairs in circulation—mine, Lorenzo's, and an agent's who field tested them. Lorenzo and I hadn't conducted tests between ourselves in two weeks because we'd both been busy on other tasks.

I accessed the messages, and there was a single message

that had no sender name attached. The message was simple:
C me

If anybody caught me staring hard into the mirror, they might think I was trying to see into Wonderland.

I focused on the words floating in front of my eyes.

Why was this familiar?

I knew this.... I just had to figure....

That's it!

I'd sent a similar message in Denver to help TOS find me. *Watch me.*

Lorenzo!

He must have his lenses in. Rather than trying to message back, I pulled the unregistered phone from the pack and called his personal number.

"Hey, it's Lorenzo...."

Straight to voicemail like yesterday. I disconnected.

I blinked the sequence of commands to bring up the lenses menu and discovered that Lorenzo's message was sent nearly three hours ago.

I brought up the screen to reply and typed *Y*. I stopped short of sending it. He'd configured his message to go out with no sender information. The reply had to be the same. If I sent it as is, it would be branded as Winger with information that could possibly be used to get my location.

I could make the same configuration changes that he did and get the message out.

Back in the main room, before I brought the computer online, I modified it further to mask its address and change it at random intervals. Last night I'd only made a few changes, but I wanted as much masking as I could to keep me stealth. I updated all my electronics to do this.

It was more difficult to do anything about the phone

number on the unregistered phone. I didn't have another SIM card, so I had to settle for changing what I could. If I kept to text messages that could transmit over the internet, it would be easier to mask my communications.

Once I was satisfied that every possible connection was secure and modified the lenses text function, I went back to Lorenzo's message and sent the Y.

If the messaging worked like it was supposed to, only Lorenzo, wearing the lenses, would be able to read it.

Hopefully he would.

Like a lightning bolt, an idea struck me.

Why hadn't I thought of this earlier?

Mom and Dad had tracking code on their phones that would be nearly impossible to remove. I'd put it there a long time ago and had only used it once—to look for Dad during the tracker case.

Sometimes I worried I'd get in serious trouble for planting the code—either my parents would somehow discover it and ground me, or TOS would come down on me for leaving a security loophole for myself. Times like this, though, it was ideal to have some insight on where they were. Or, at least where the phone was.

Opening a command prompt, I typed the simple commands to find Dad. After a few moments of a spinning cursor, a set of coordinates appeared. I routed my Google Maps session through a web anonymizer and revealed Dad's location to be Potsdam, Germany. He'd been on a mission, so I didn't know if he was supposed to be there, but it wouldn't be out of the question.

Mom's phone pinged back even faster showing her in Victoria, British Columbia—not far from her last known location. Getting out of the States might have been the right call for her.

The message icon flashed in the lenses. Despite using these for testing, the alert jarred me. I looked to it, so it would open.

Alone?

Again the sender was unnamed, but it *had* to be Lorenzo.

I typed back: Y

I waited. Time slowed to the point that each second felt infinite. Since I responded right back, he would surely keep up the conversation.

Accept feed?

We'd barely begun to test the video overlay capability in this release of the lenses. It allowed agents working together to see what the other could see in a picture-in-picture setup.

As soon as I accepted, a rectangle opened across the upper right quadrant of my vision. I'd only tested this once before, and it was disorienting having a video on top of normal vision, especially since I could see through it and around it.

The view was an open laptop screen with a blank word processing page. Letters formed as someone typed.

It's Doc.

The typing paused for a moment and then continued.

Standby.

The picture bounced as Lorenzo moved. It was impossible to tell what he was doing. His phone suddenly appeared, and he swiped to his camera app. Flipping the camera around, his face appeared on the screen.

My heartbeat pounded in my ears as butterflies bounced off the walls of my stomach. It was hard to not surrender to the rush of emotion at seeing the first trusted face in so many hours.

It quickly sunk in, though, that he was hurt. An angry

purple bruise extended along the left side of his face and his upper lip was split and puffy. Somehow, he managed a slight smile, though, as he waved at the screen. He propped the phone against the computer screen so I could see his face as he typed.

Can you do video?

I responded: Y

I blinked my way through the menu to open the link, so he'd be able to see. While the link established, I set up everything like he did—I loved being able to type on the computer for him to see instead of having to form the words with my eyes. Once the green icon lit up to indicate we were connected, I waved back at him. He shuddered and looked like he couldn't decide to laugh or cry. I understood 100 percent.

Are you okay? You look rough.

He shrugged and typed back: *HQ was overrun yesterday evening. A few of us managed to avoid capture. I'm trying to restore the network. What about you?*

This was worse than I could've imagined.

I typed: *I'm okay. House was breached. I got away. Shotgun is badly injured...maybe worse.*

I wiped at my eyes after I typed that, hoping to beat back the emotion that rose up.

The shock on Lorenzo's face said everything. He hadn't known. I wanted to ask him if he knew anything about Mom and Dad, but it didn't seem right.

Can I help with network?

Lorenzo's shrug and eye roll said it all.

I thought I had it earlier, but I either tripped a security protocol or someone monitoring shut me down. I've located Amp and Ghostlight, but they're on the move looking for a secure place to be. If you're somewhere

Lorenzo jerked his head to look behind him, and he slammed the laptop shut.

The feed went dark before I could see who found him.

I quickly closed the connection on my side just in case.

"Please don't be dead," I murmured to the empty room.

EIGHT

I'D STEPPED AWAY from the computer for a while after what had happened to Lorenzo. If I thought it was safe, I'd have gone for a walk to clear my head. Instead, I lay back on the bed. I drifted between thinking about the past day and the clues I might have, dozing and jerking back awake when images of John or Lorenzo forced their way in.

After an hour or so, I returned to the desk.

While Lorenzo confirmed the TOS network had been compromised, some things continued to work right. For the text and video of the lenses to work, a connection was established, and I needed to exploit that.

Had he tried accessing the network that way? Or was it something he'd restored and didn't have time to tell me? It was worth a try to see if I could make some progress that way.

The logs the lenses would've recorded provided a good place to start. Copies of all lens activity went to my secure cloud because of the debugging I'd been working on.

The lenses operated along the same network path they

always did. Whatever had hijacked most of the network hadn't affected this.

Using the log information, I'd connected directly to the interface that controlled the lenses. I'd hesitated at the login because if anyone caught it, they'd see I'd done it. I should have enough measures in place that my physical location wouldn't be revealed.

The question became: How far could I get? Opening up another couple of windows, it was annoying that I only had the one small laptop screen because there was so much I needed to see simultaneously.

While I enjoyed moving through the system outside of the slick user interface, I hated wasting the time. Traffic was almost nonexistent, indicating exactly how incapacitated the network was.

There had to be—

The unregistered phone vibrated on the desktop, and I pushed back from the desk so hard I almost knocked the chair over.

No number or name displayed on the screen. The caller knew how to mask their number, location, and caller ID.

I swiped to connect the call but said nothing as I held the phone to my ear.

Seconds ticked by.

TOS protocol dictated the other side speak first and identify. While we weren't on a secure line, I wanted the caller to go first.

"Come on, Theo. Don't you want to say hello?"

The voice was familiar, but I couldn't immediately place it.

I stayed quiet. They didn't have to know that I'd picked up. Someone else could have this phone.

"Would you rather I said, Winger, Westside here."

Fuck.

How did he get this number?

I trembled like I'd fallen through the ice on a pond. Westside had taunted me in Denver, and my fingers trembled at the thought of punishing him for this.

He'd been one of the Blackbird agents responsible for hacking into the TOS agent tracking system and capturing Dad. He'd been taken into custody in Denver, but he'd escaped. His wife had worked undercover at Glenwood Music to infect audio files with code that could steal people's personal information and emit a sound that could drive certain people, myself included, into a rage.

"We both know you're trying to decide on something clever to say. But you've got no moves. We've got the TOS network. We've got many of your colleagues. Maybe more importantly we know where Victor and Katherine are. Or, if you'd prefer protocol, Defender and Snowbird. Should we just call them Mom and Dad? Your pick. We'll have them in the next few hours." He sounded cocky with his sickeningly sweet voice.

What had I done to let this happen? Security was one of my priorities. Somehow I'd let everyone down.

Was it because Eddie got my computer in New York? Everyone thought the computer had been fried before any information could be accessed.

I punched at the air with my free hand and kicked at the garbage can, sending it flying across the room toward the front door. Its meager contents of a couple of napkins scattered across the floor.

"It's time you figured out we're the right team. It would've been so much easier if you'd been home when we showed up yesterday. You might have convinced John to cooperate."

He disconnected.

The phone slipped from my hand and bounced off the edge of the desk. I tried to catch it but missed, and it fell to the floor.

I gulped for air as my chest tightened.

Truth or deception?

It seemed inconceivable that every TOS agent could be captured in less than twenty-four hours. I didn't have a timeline on when things started going bad, but if it started with John yesterday it had only been sixteen or seventeen hours.

A command line window opened on the computer.

Maybe you'd rather talk here instead. What are you up to Theo?

The cursor blinked after the question mark.

War Games, *Tron*, and *Mr. Robot* flashed through my mind.

Rather than answer, I checked the security on the phone and laptop and everything looked like I was on the internet from Waco, Texas and Boulder, Colorado.

I could sever the connection, but that wouldn't yield anything.

Trying to hide the fact that I'd logged in was ridiculous since I'd used my credentials.

Enough.

It was time to battle back. Westside and Blackbird had to pay for what they'd done to John, Lorenzo, and everyone else.

I typed: *Just trying to find out what you've done and fix it.*

In another window, I continued exploring the network, looking for signs of why it was offline. If Blackbird was rounding up agents, they had to be using the communications and tracker network to find them. That meant there had to be a way to access those systems—and likely more.

Why don't you let us pick you up? We can show you exactly what we've done. Maybe you can convince Lorenzo to join us. He's being a stubborn holdout—a lot like you.

From the set of tools I had in cloud storage, I deployed some reconnaissance bots to look around and report back, specifically on inbound and outbound network traffic.

Depending on what I learned, another possibility would be to send out bots to overwhelm the system. If I put too much stress on it, I could force a reboot that might allow me to regain full control.

You realize you're just one person, right? There's no way you can get past the army of people we've got making sure we stay in control.

Almost as if Blackbird had jinxed itself, I found a path courtesy of one of the bots and lenses. The data stream from the lenses was tiny because of how we compressed it. Like the trackers and comms, it was stealth by design so that it could travel along various networks and be undetected except by the most sensitive monitoring systems.

I piggybacked on the data to get into the larger network. *You've always underestimated me, Westside.*

There it was. I gained access to the full network.

"Yes!" I shouted into the empty room

Let me know when you've changed your mind. We're not going to wait much longer.

I rolled my eyes. Maybe he wasn't—

The screen went dark.

What did he do?

There'd been no sign that he'd locked on to me.

I held the power button down until I heard the hard disc power down. I counted to ten before powering back up.

Nothing. Just a white screen.

I powered down again and took the extra step of unplugging the power cord and counted to ten again.

I tried to boot up in safe mode.

Once again, nothing but white.

Shit.

He'd fried the laptop—just like I'd tried to do with the electronics they stole yesterday.

I slammed the lid down and shoved it across the desk.

So stupid. I'd taken so many precautions, and yet I hadn't disabled the code to allow the laptop to be fried.

My best weapon to fight with was gone.

I'd truly messed this up.

NINE

ONCE I'D BEATEN back the frustration, I checked the computer again. It was truly dead. When TOS blacklisted electronics, they had to go back to HQ for refurbishment if they were going to be reused.

That wasn't an option.

Mom told me once that it was nearly impossible to account for every scenario. One of the things TOS liked about my work was that I often thought outside the box to get things done. Maybe if I'd been more methodical in this case, I wouldn't have lost the computer.

A new one, with the power I required to do the necessary work, would cost more than I'd want to spend. They could be had cheaper online but waiting on shipping was out of the question too.

A public computer would be too risky because it wouldn't be secure enough.

With my MIT student ID, I might be able to talk my way into a computer lab at any of the nearby universities. But that would likely get logged in to a system that Blackbird might catch. I should've had a student ID made up for my new identity. I'd add that to the list of things that had gone wrong in this operation.

There was no choice but to spend the money. I had to have a computer, and it would take way too much time to figure out how to steal one.

Did I have Blackbird fooled that I'd left Boston?

If I were them, I'd assume that I'd secure another computer. It probably didn't matter if I bought it with a card that had my real name. I'd just have to get away from the store as quickly as possible, so they couldn't easily pick me up.

I didn't trust my ability to stay under the radar at this hotel. I'd screwed up letting them take out the computer. I might have missed something else.

I gathered up what few things I'd taken out of my pack. Out the window, nothing looked suspicious. I left the key card in the room and headed for my parked bike. At least I had transportation.

Maps showed me that a Best Buy was less than a mile away.

Biking on the busy street in broad daylight put a ball of stress in my stomach. I couldn't hide, and the bike helmet obscured me only so much. Once I removed that, I had no other cover.

Blackbird wasn't stupid. They'd be monitoring the cams.

I'd plan better before I went out again.

Best Buy had a few customers and several employees. Keeping my head downcast would help avoid identification. As I headed toward the computers at the back of the store, Mitch's team picture displayed on the wall of TVs to my right. Under it were the words "breaking news."

What?

I froze in the middle of the aisle transfixed. Iris's picture from last year's yearbook replaced Mitch's.

No. No. No. A vise locked on to my chest, and it felt like my heart might implode.

My team picture flashed on the screen next. I was totally exposed now in the store. Salespeople watched the screens, and it would only be a matter of time before one of them saw me.

A photo of John came up next to mine. I'd never seen this one. It looked like a snapshot from a phone, maybe. He was in a T-shirt, outside, smiling as if he had no cares.

Dizziness overtook me, and I grabbed on to the shelf of cell phone accessories to stay upright. I took the necessary deep breaths to not pass out. The story ended, and anchors were back on the screen. Under them was an 800-number asking for people to call with any tips.

TOS would've covered all this up. Me and John in the news wouldn't be allowed. How did Mitch and Iris factor in?

It couldn't be good.

Thankfully the computer department was on the other side of the store although the TVs were still visible. Until I knew what that story said, I needed an even lower profile.

A couple of dozen computers were set out on counters. I didn't bother with the ones under a thousand dollars— they wouldn't have the computing power. Quickly finding one that looked good, I got out of the demo screen to learn more about the configurations than what the tag on the front said.

"Can I help you with anything? Any questions about that model?"

"No. I think I'm good."

"You do seem to know your stuff since you're looking at

all the system information. What exactly do you plan to use it for? I can help pick the best one."

Even under normal circumstances, I didn't need a salesperson talking to me about what to buy. I usually configured online and had units shipped if it was for purely personal use. Tech I used for TOS work came customized from the organization to meet its security requirements.

"Nope. No questions. I'll take one of these." I put the computer back into its demo mode so that the next person could be dazzled by the flashy presentation.

This guy looked way too happy. He was either still hopped up on his morning coffee or enjoyed his job a whole bunch.

"We do have a couple sales if you want to change to—"

"No, thanks. I want this one." I pointed at the tag. "And I don't care about the color. Whatever you can put in my hands right now."

Holding back the frustration took massive amounts of patience I didn't really have. Playing the role of a customer looking for help, however, did not work its way into my schedule.

"Or you can really amp up the processing power for just five hundred—"

"This is exactly what I need. Can you please get it for me, so I can get going?"

The clerk, whose name tag read "Ian" looked like I'd deflated him. Maybe he had a script he needed to go through. "Let me go to the back and grab one. Do you need anything else? Portable drives, extra battery packs or anything?"

"Nope," I said, trying to sound more cheerful. "Just the computer. Mine died on me this morning, and I've got too much work to do."

That got him on his way.

While he got the computer, I became enthralled with all the types of mouse I could buy. Anything to keep from looking toward the TVs.

He was back with the box quickly. I followed him to the register.

"Can I interest you in two years of extended warranty?"

"No, thanks. If anything goes wrong, I'll just get a new one."

He shrugged, and I hoped he was done with his chatter.

He scanned the box and told me the nearly $2,000 total. I flashed him one of my cards and he tapped on his screen.

"Not this again." More tapping on the screen and the connected keyboard had him frowning. I couldn't see what was wrong. It couldn't be my card since he hadn't swiped it yet. "I'm sorry, sir. Just one moment. The system has been having issues on and off all morning."

I gave him a nod as he gave me the worried look of a cashier who feared a transaction may not complete. He pushed a few more keys and his smile returned. "Okay, back to normal. I hope someone's looking into this. Otherwise it's going to be a very long day."

I put the chip card in the reader, and it authorized fast. In short order I had the receipt in my hand, the box under my arm and was headed out the door only to be stopped one last time by the guard, checking to make sure that I'd actually paid for it.

Back on the sidewalk, I exhaled relieved to have gotten out of there without being tied to the news report.

How many people saw it? It must've been big to interrupt programming. Maybe I shouldn't have checked out of the hotel because going anywhere else now could be a problem. I might even be at more risk on the street than if just Blackbird was looking for me.

There was a Starbucks across the street, and it'd be as good a place as any to look up what the story was.

Many of the tables were filled with people on laptops, and no one looked up as I came in. Thankfully there were no TVs in here. I got a bottle of water and a muffin before dropping into one of the few open seats. I was adjacent to the front window, but I wasn't facing out. The most the street could see was my profile.

WBZ News was usually my first stop for local info. I almost dropped the phone reading the headline across the top of the homepage.

Two McKinley high students assaulted, one abducted

Below the headline were the images I'd seen of Mitch and Iris.

Everything seemed to tilt, and I closed my eyes for a moment. I couldn't get sick or freak out here.

Around eleven thirty this morning, two McKinley High students were assaulted and one abducted from the campus parking lot. Mitchell Rhodes and Iris Lancaster were leaving campus for lunch when a van that had been making a routine delivery to the school's cafeteria detoured and forced them into the vehicle. Lancaster managed to escape when students and school officials intervened. Rhodes, however, was taken off campus.

Jesus.

There was no way this wasn't Blackbird. And they didn't let Iris make a lucky escape. If they wanted her, they'd have her.

I braced myself and clicked the "read more" link.

My pictures and John's were on this page.

Police are looking for any information that can lead to the recovery of Rhodes.

It's unknown if this abduction is connected to the overnight story of a possible homicide. Following an anonymous 911 call, police were dispatched to the home of seventeen-year-old McKinley student Theodore Reese. At the residence, John Keller was found dead. Police are looking for Reese, who was seen entering the home before the 911 call came in. Reese's parents, Victor and Katherine Reese, are also unaccounted for so police are asking for assistance in locating the young man.

Persons with any information related to the whereabouts of Rhodes, Reese, Reese's parents, or any connections between these incidents are asked to call the Boston Police Department tip line.

The shakes got worse, and I gripped both sides of the phone to keep it from jumping out of my hands. They couldn't go after my friends and not expect me to do something.

Ignoring my surroundings, I unpacked the laptop and started setting it up. Unusual for a coffee shop, sure. But if I was going to reestablish a base camp, I needed it online.

Waiting through the setup screens was tedious, I didn't even need most of what was moving across the screen. I skipped as much of it as I could. After an excruciatingly long ten minutes, I opened the system window and logged on to our family's cloud. Nothing immediately looked out of place, which was either because it hadn't been found or because it was being monitored. Hopefully I'd secured it well enough that it was the former.

I pulled the tools I needed, only grabbing what I required. These apps, scripts, and other tools were a mix of

TOS-approved items along with ones I'd been working on that weren't yet ready for the agency.

I didn't use my skills to do anything illegal. One of the reasons I specialized in cybersecurity was because I believed data integrity and security was integral to modern life. The current extraordinary circumstances forced me to break my usual rules.

Google Maps showed me the nearby hotels. There were quite a few, and it didn't take me long to find one that had what I needed. It was just three blocks away, and it used digital keys, which allowed guests to open doors with phone apps.

Perfect!

I went to the hotel's website and went through the steps to book a room. Tracing the data flow, I saw the path to the reservation system. Back over in the command window, I unleashed a couple of my best scripts to go poke around and find the way in.

Since I didn't want to be caught on the cameras that watched the registration desk and I didn't want to swipe any of my cards, going in through the digital backdoor provided a secure method to get a room and, in this case, even a key.

The security around the reservation system was decent, but I broke in quickly and got myself a room, free Wi-Fi, and the electronic key that would appear as soon as I down-loaded the app.

Trickier than creating the reservation that would let me stay for a week, however, was paying for it. I wasn't going to steal the room, but I did write an elaborate script to take cash out of my personal checking account and made it look like it paid several online merchants. That money got routed to the hotel in what looked like a single card swipe from a new alter ego since I didn't know if Jason Karr was compromised or not. I'd even made it appear that the room had been booked and paid for three months ago. This was as safe as I could make it.

As long as I stayed smart, I should be able to keep this hideout.

TEN

I WANTED to see Iris in person, but there'd be so many cops, and likely other law enforcement agencies, around her family that getting near her would be impossible even if I wasn't also a wanted person.

I'd have to settle for texting. Although I'd probably have to convince her it was me since I'd be on the other end of an anonymous number. If that failed, I'd risk showing up.

As soon as the computer was online, I opened the command window to do something I hadn't done in years—sending an SMS text message with no identifying information. I used to prank Mitch with all kinds of weird texts. It was fun when I was thirteen.

In this case it would help keep Iris and me safe. I customized this program to ensure no traces would be left.

Iris wasn't someone who kept her phone close at all times. Hopefully with everything going on, though, she'd have hers nearby to get news.

Once the program was done, I sent a couple of test messages back and forth with my unsecured phone. Everything seemed to work perfectly. Looking at the phone diagnostics, there was no indication a text message had ever come in. I used a valid Boston area code so Iris would recognize it, but the only place the reply could go was back to the computer.

Iris? It's Theo. Type back to me. This message will disappear in fifteen seconds, or when you start typing. Whichever happens first.

I waited.

Too much time passed.

I sent the same message again.

In just a couple seconds, the dots appeared indicating her typing.

Theo? This isn't your number. How do I know it's you?

I saw the news. Are you okay? You can ask me anything to help prove it's me.

I don't know what's happening, Theo. Can I even trust you? If it's you?

I know it's been crazy. I didn't want to freak her out worse. I also didn't know how much to say, but I really didn't have much to lose. *I want to help get Mitch back.*

The seconds ticked by and just when I was sure she wasn't going to respond, the dots appeared. She typed for a long time. I imagined her writing and then erasing to start again.

What's the only movie that made all four of us cry?

Great question.

Despite everything going on, it stabbed at my heart to remember all of us going to see *Love, Simon.* Eddie always got emotional first, followed by either me or Iris. Mitch wasn't a crier, unless it was a particularly moving death scene. We all lost it when Simon and his mom had their big talk after he'd come out.

I answered.

God, Theo. It is you. It all happened so fast. We were headed to my car to drive out for lunch and these men crossed the parking lot toward us. Mitch didn't hesitate to step in front of me because these guys looked bad.

Of course he'd moved to protect her. Although I imagined her trying to do the same to him. She didn't take anyone's crap.

God, I'd brought this on my friends. How could I keep them safe?

And I knew how terrifying this could be.

I battled against my emotions to keep them in check. The focus had to be getting Mitch home.

A van sped in, and they grabbed both of us. They yanked him in, but they let me go and gave me a message for you. You need to text Mitch's name to 946437. How is that even something that works?

It was a clever way to make me talk to them.

A white-hot ball of fury built in my chest—like lava ready to burst from a volcano. They'd come after my friends, my family. Everyone.

How do they know you, Theo? First you're not at school, and then this. And I saw the news. Are you okay?

Jesus, I could only imagine what she must be thinking.

I wanted to hug her and tell her this would be okay. As angry as I'd become getting the story, it ripped me up to know I was the cause. The only reason they were targeted was because of the work I did.

I sucked as a friend.

I'm okay. I will get Mitch back. I promise.

No other outcome could be accepted.

Is it true about John?

A sad sigh escaped while I stared at the screen deciding what to say.

I don't know.

I truly didn't. Not only could I not take a news report's word for anything, I also hoped with every fiber of my being that he would be okay.

Can I see you, Theo? Only for a minute. Just to know, you know.

I thought quickly. The interface I was on wouldn't let me send a photo. FaceTime would be too traceable, and it would take too long to hack a solution for that.

Are you near your computer?

I knew how we could do this and not get caught.

No. The police are here and looking at my computer. They've already been over my phone. Don't worry about it. I had to ask. Will you let me know how it goes?

You'll know it worked out when Mitch gets back.

What about you?

What about me? I didn't know what to tell her. First priority was Mitch's recovery. Then I either had to connect with TOS or I had to go after Westside. Maybe those two things went together.

Theo?

You're freaking me out.

I had nothing to lose with the truth.

I don't know. I need to go get Mitch. Be safe, Iris. Know that I'm going to do everything I can.

Don't you dare stop talking to me. Come home with him, Theo.

I closed the connection. I couldn't bear to see what she'd type next. While I didn't know what would happen to me, I suspected that was my last time to talk to Iris.

Dropping my head into my hands, I wanted that to not be true. Iris and Mitch meant the world to me—as much as Eddie had. I couldn't lose them too.

I tried to shove my emotions into a box. I had no clue what to think.

Not being able to see my friends again was worth it if it meant I stopped Blackbird from doing something terrible. Spock was always right about the needs of the many.

How did agents manage all the risk? My parents worried about me getting into the TOS world so early. The work I did helped people, and I enjoyed most of it, even though it sometimes scared me. What was the cost, though?

Iris and Mitch didn't deserve to be caught up in this.

For now I had no options. Using the interface I'd texted Iris on, I followed the instructions she provided.

There was no lag time in the reply. *We've got Mitch and, except for convincing him not to fight, he's okay. If he behaves we'll feed him dinner later.*

They kept typing.

It's curious how you sent this message. Obviously not a real Boston phone number and we can't get a trace either. Well done.

I worked furiously to track them. The data indicated they used a standard Galaxy S8 phone. With the short code, I expected the response to come back from a computer. Of course, they could be masking like I was.

What do I need to do to get Mitch released?

Their transmission came from an IP originating in Warrendale. If that was true, they weren't far from me.

Coordinates appeared on screen.

Your loyalty to your captain is admirable, and exactly what we hoped for. You need to turn yourself over and start working with us. You have two hours to get to the address above. And before you tell us that you can't get here in two hours, we know where you bought your computer and you can't be too far from there.

The morning's mistake kept coming back to haunt me.

How do I know you're going to keep your word?

You don't. We know your reputation, though. You're not going to risk Mitch. Don't forget: We can always go back for Iris.

Of course they would.

Okay. You win.

I closed the connection because I'd heard enough.

Maps showed the location was five miles away. I could bike there in less than thirty minutes, so I had time to sort out a plan.

ELEVEN

Before I left the hotel, there was one stop to make. In the lobby giftshop, I bought a pair of cheap sunglasses—far bigger than I would normally buy—and a baseball cap. It would look weird if I had my hood up all the time, but people wear caps indoors and out, and it would cover most of my red hair. I stuffed the glasses and cap into my pack, which I'd kept as light as possible by leaving clothes in the room.

Food.

Damn. I'd left that muffin and water behind, no wonder my stomach rumbled.

After I'd unlocked my bike, a news notification pinged on my watch. I couldn't ignore the headline: "Internet Outages Plague US, EU."

On the phone, I flipped over to my news app and the top story was about random internet outages that had been happening for the past day plaguing sites, entire providers, and even private networks. At this point there was no information about cause and each issue seemed to clear up within a few minutes.

Blackbird. It couldn't be a coincidence that they moved on TOS at the same time these outages occurred.

Traffic was light, so the ride to the park was easy. I locked up the bike and helmet on the first rack I found. I wasted no time in getting the sunglasses and hat on.

A playground at one corner had the most activity with younger kids having afterschool playtime. Elsewhere some people my age or older played Frisbee and others walked around with dogs or in small groups talking. Nothing appeared out of the ordinary.

I went to an empty picnic table and was happy to see someone else with their laptop and a coffee preferring the fall afternoon outdoors to being in a coffee shop. It made it less weird that I pulled my laptop out.

I planned to spend thirty to forty-five minutes in the park seeing if I could infiltrate the building and affect a rescue. I wanted Mitch free. While they could recapture him, I hoped that he'd be safe with Boston police back home.

I'd used Google Street View to examine the building and surroundings as best as I could before I left the hotel and luckily nothing had changed since Google's last drive-by. Three plain stories with tinted windows—a drab office building. No exterior signage save for the address stenciled on the glass over the door. The front door was steel with no window and a simple handle. As I passed on my bike, I saw a keypad as well. That small detail wasn't on Google.

I had tried to get Street View for around the building, but apparently the Google car hadn't gone down the alleys on the side or back of the building. The satellite view didn't provide useful details.

What was going on inside? The lenses could help figure

this out. I accessed the menu and viewed the electrical currents.

Out here there were a lot of currents to see from the buildings, traffic signals, underground and above ground electrical wires, and even the tiny energy readings from cell phones and other devices in people's pockets. I went back to the menu and selected the zoom option.

Zoom was my least favorite mode. It was bizarre having my vision get closer to something without moving. The lens design let me draw a box around the part I wanted closeup, and it would come forward. Everything else stayed as it would normally appear, letting agents keep their peripheral vision. I found it disorienting, but the field testers reported liking it.

The building used a tremendous amount of electricity, particularly the back half of the first floor. Perhaps it was some sort of data center. I couldn't see exactly what was happening, but it looked like electricity flowed to things that were stacked up, which would be consistent with server racks. The rest of the building had a more standard flow, with what was likely electrical outlets and lighting.

More important to me than the energy flow was data. I switched the lens from looking at energy to fiber optics. The amount of fiber optic activity on the first floor validated my hypothesis on the energy usage—it had to be a cluster of servers. Were they running the internet disruptions from here? Or was this something else? TOS kept its systems distributed around the world, so this could be one part of an elaborate network.

Next, I looked at the Wi-Fi signals. The building was covered in it—all one network, but there were six repeaters on each floor. I didn't see spots with no coverage.

Since I'd taken possession of these new lenses a few

weeks ago, I used this function a lot. Studying Wi-Fi networks in public spaces fascinated me, especially seeing the names they had. Every time I found an unsecure one, I fought the urge to tell the owner to fix that. So many networks crossed my vision now, but it was easy to home in on the one that I wanted because of the built-in color coding —each network had its own color.

The lenses gathered information about the hubs, so I had the names and IP addresses. Combining the Wi-Fi and fiber optic information, I could see how it all worked together from a single source.

I didn't want to connect to any of the Wi-Fi hubs. Blackbird no doubt had those well secured.

Getting inside the building was the way to go. I could get Mitch out and then find a place to hardwire into their system.

Returning the contacts to normal vision, I connected the laptop to the park's Wi-Fi and made the computer look like it was in Kansas City. This would be easier if I could see the data flow as I worked, so I engaged that on my left eye while leaving my right with normal vision. I stared at the building and waited for my eyes to adjust.

I found a second data connection I hadn't seen originally because it had far less traffic. Another IP came into the building and didn't appear to go into the main servers, but it did run throughout the building. I sent in some bots to explore the new address, which was an open connection.

Security used this, and it was connected to cameras, card readers, and a couple of fingerprint readers.

Perfect.

I discovered the master security control panel. Why this was accessible from the outside baffled me, but doors could be accidentally left ajar and I was lucky enough to find this one.

Or maybe luck had nothing to do with it. A trap, perhaps?

They wanted me here and maybe they thought I'd walk in the front door. But I had no intention of turning myself over without knowing Mitch was safe. So, it didn't matter why this loophole existed because I had no choice but to exploit it.

Dozens of security cameras covered the building inside and out. I brought up a grid of those to look around. Immediately I looked close at the external cameras and breathed a sigh of relief that I was not on camera from my position in the park. The cameras mostly watched over the immediate sidewalk around the building. Inside a single larger room ten people worked—some at whiteboards and others at terminals. Elsewhere I found a couple of dozen other people in smaller groups. I didn't see Westside anywhere. Of course there could be an area with no cameras and lots more people, but given the data, it didn't seem likely. I studied each room with people individually.

Mitch!

I'd envisioned him being bound to a chair with a gag stuffed in his mouth—a byproduct of too many movies. Instead he paced in a small room. He sported a swollen eye and a cut on his cheek that had a butterfly bandage on it. That must've happened in the fight Westside had alluded to.

Where was he in the building? There were no windows in his room, so he'd be on an interior hallway or facing the building next door.

Looking through the control interface I found a floor plan that indicated camera location. Camera H35 was on the second floor. Now I had a map of the building. With the TOS phone, I snapped pictures of the floor plans. There were two exterior doors, the one in the front, facing the street and one in the far back corner. The map let me confirm that there were few spots inside the building that weren't covered by cameras.

What was on the roof? The building next door was tall enough and close enough that I could jump over if there was an entry up there.

I pulled up Google Satellite. With the image I could line up what I saw on the roof with the plans I'd acquired and find a way in.

TWELVE

THE BUILDING next door to Blackbird was full of professional offices, and it was easy to walk in and go upstairs. The guard didn't seem to care where I was going, which was perfect.

The stairs went up to the roof where the door was ajar. I expected maybe an alarmed door, some kind of fire exit. Of course, this door could be like this all the time. I took a breath, ready to deal with whoever I might find on the other side.

Apparently, the roof was an often-used area. A place for smokers stood away from the door with a couple of ash cans. A small deck sat to one side, complete with a pergola and two picnic tables. Thankfully no one was on break. I didn't want an audience who might call the cops on the kid jumping between buildings.

The gap between the buildings was about ten feet and from this high my heart leapt in my chest a little bit as I surveyed the space. It'd been a long time since I had to do a long jump, probably back in elementary school phys ed. I knew a guy on the McKinley track team who long jumped twenty plus feet. Surely, I could do half since falling three stories wasn't something I wanted to try. I'd been getting some TOS field training over the past year, and I mentally added some instruction on this kind of scenario to my to-do list.

My heart thumped hard as I backed up to get a running start. I took off, ran a dozen or so feet, and leapt right at the edge, pushing off as hard as I could with my right foot.

Crossing the gap, I swallowed a scream. I thought about contestants on *American Ninja Warrior* who misstepped and ended up in the water.

I hit the roof on the other side, bending my legs to absorb some of the impact. Once I stopped, I exhaled in relief.

As I'd seen on the satellite view, there was a small, closet-sized area where the door went into one of the main staircases. Hopefully it was unguarded—and no one was on a break.

Adjusting the lenses, I went to heat-vision mode to see if anyone would appear. This function had given us the most trouble to implement, especially when used outdoors. I quickly saw what they meant because there were patterns all over my vision and none of them looked like a person. Clearly still a work-in-progress. Exiting from heat vision, I moved across the roof as stealthily as I could. Each time my shoes crunched on the tar and gravel surface, I flinched and tried to walk lighter.

"Stop where you are." The voice came from my left, and I froze.

Crap.

"Winger?" I recognized the voice, and I was as surprised as they sounded.

"D-Man?" I asked as I turned slowly.

He holstered his gun under his coat, and we stepped forward to embrace. Thank God.

I hugged him tight—tighter than I probably should've, but I was thrilled to finally see a friend and colleague.

"My God, I'm happy to see you," I said, my voice breaking as I released him.

"I've no idea what's going on. I followed Mitch to this location after he was taken. I saw the news about…. Is it true about Shotgun?"

I shrugged and felt the sting of tears the thought of John triggered. "I hope I got him help in time… but he ordered me to go."

Coach nodded and drew me into another hug, which I happily accepted.

"Do you know about anyone else?" I said with my face plastered against his shoulder. I didn't name specific names, news of anyone would be good at this point.

"Snowbird contacted me last night and told me you were on the move. When I got to your house there were a ton of police. I knew you'd been there, but you covered your tracks well. I haven't been able to reach anyone from TOS in—" He looked at his watch. "—nearly a day now."

"I'm here for Mitch too. They left a message with Iris. I'm supposed to turn myself in or they'll hurt him."

"I wondered why they didn't make more of an effort to take her. They knew you'd see the news and get in touch with her."

I nodded. "They want me. I've had conversations with Westside. Remember him?" Coach looked shocked but nodded. "He fried my computer earlier today when I wouldn't do what he wanted and then he upped the pressure. So, do you have a plan for getting into this place?"

Coach shrugged and rolled his eyes in a combination

that under other circumstances would've made me laugh. "I figured the roof was better than the front door, and I was just going to go for it because sometimes that's all you can do. What about you?"

"I've got a few ideas." I squatted and pulled off my backpack to get the laptop. "I gathered intel from across the street. It's better than nothing, I imagine." I walked him through what I had.

"I'm going to use the camera interface to create a loop on the stairwell cameras. It's dark, and it'll be easy to do. I can't do that to all of them. Most of the other cameras show people. I pushed the security console to my phone so I'll be able to look at individual cameras as we move, and I might be able to manipulate some of them. It depends on what's in view."

"That plan is about as good as it gets. At least we'll have eyes. Ready when you are." It took a couple minutes longer than I'd anticipated to get the video to accept a five-second-infinite loop as the input for the stairwell cameras, but I felt pretty sure that I hadn't alerted anybody. I wanted to do the same thing to the camera in Mitch's room. But he never stopped pacing, and I couldn't risk any stuttering glitches.

"What do you know about this door?" I looked to Coach for the answer. Maybe he'd studied how to get in before I got here. I packed the laptop away as he talked.

"It looks like a regular fire exit. If it's up to code, there'll be an alarm on it. But if it's like so many that I've seen, the alarm's disabled to allow people to come up and chill." He gestured with his head to the building next door. "You saw the one over there—not secure at all."

"Let me see what's around this door." I changed one of the lenses to show me data and electric flow. "It looks like there's a door sensor as well as one in the locking mechanism."

"Who are you with this x-ray vision?"

I got another surprised look as I pointed out the exact spots.

"Luckily when Blackbird ransacked my room, they didn't get everything." I didn't go into a ton of details because these lenses were still classified.

"I don't think the app that I'd normally use to disrupt alarm current around the door will work given the network outage."

I considered a moment. Trying to hack the alarm would take longer than I wanted to spend. "Give it a shot. Many of the apps don't need the network."

He pulled out his phone, unlocked it and flipped through a couple screens. "All right. Point out where those sensors are again."

He put the phone up to the door, read the display, and tapped the screen. I didn't recognize the app other than it had some design features common among TOS apps. Coach tapped the screen and the energy flow changed so it bypassed the door sensor and created a loop.

"One down. Where's the other?"

I pointed out the one that was near the latch.

If we got out of this, I'd have to find out how that worked. Redirecting the energy flow like that without a disruption was clever. The second one took longer, but he ultimately succeeded.

"Nice of you guys to design for a little resiliency. Just in case." He put the phone away. "Now we go old-school."

He pulled out a small leather pouch and bounced it a couple times in his hands. Unzipping it, he retrieved what he needed to pick the lock.

It took less than thirty seconds by my count for the lock to click. We smiled about the small victory.

"Any idea what's on the other side of the door?"

"Stairwell with doors at each level and, it's a safe bet, sensors on the doors. There are cameras on each floor and on both sides of the door.

Coach repackaged his picks. "And Mitch?"

"Second floor. Four doors down from the stairwell." I used the phone to show what was outside Mitch's door. "The hallway doesn't have too much activity, but there is this one guy who must be assigned to guard him."

He nodded. "Did you have a plan for dealing with him?"

"Nope." I shrugged. "I figured I'd make it up when I got there."

"If the hallway stays empty, maybe I can be the distraction you need."

"Two on one is better than one on one." It felt like a weight had lifted off my shoulders with Coach here. I hoped I was making the right choices, but having someone else to work with made this feel a lot more under control. "At least we have an idea what we're walking into." I held up my phone since that was our window into what was inside. "Let's do this."

Coach took the lead. It was standard protocol for senior agents plus they were expected to offer protection for techs, and in this case, I welcomed it.

The staircase flooded with light as we entered. Not knowing much about what was below, I hoped the light didn't travel far. None of the cameras showed activity on the stairs. I made sure the door didn't make noise as it closed.

We moved slowly down. The door on the third floor had

a small vertical window that looked into the hall. Coach saw nothing as he looked through.

Coach looked down to the next floor and he motioned for us to keep going. I held the railing as we descended since I was watching the monitors on the phone.

The second floor still showed one in the hall except Mitch's guard. All of the doors were closed, and at least the ones I saw on the monitors didn't have windows. What each of them did have was some kind of keypad or card reader.

From below, a door clanked open and then shut followed by voices of at least two people. Coach held up his hand in a fist, signaling we should stop. My heart somersaulted as a flock of butterflies cut through my stomach.

With the limited space on my phone screen, I'd been focused on the second floor, but I quickly changed my view to look at all the cams and zoomed in on the one for the staircase.

A man and women were on their way up. If they didn't go directly into the second floor, they'd see us. I pulled on Coach's jacket, hoping he'd understand to back up.

We retreated far enough that they didn't see us when they went through the second-floor door. Changing camera views again, I watched the two go into a room just across from where Mitch was. They also seemed to say hello to the guard.

"Okay," Coach said softly. "We can't stop this time."

I nodded. "It looks about as clear as it's ever gonna get."

We nodded and went to the second-floor door.

I took a moment to check for any energy signatures or data flow around the door and found none. Coach tried the push bar and it easily moved.

"Keep an eye on the screen. I'm going to do something" —by the sound of his voice he was extremely unsure what that something was going to be—"to take care of that guard so you can get in. What will you do about the reader at the door?"

"Let me see?"

I nudged him aside to look out the stairwell window. Across the hall was a keycard reader and I didn't have a tool for that with me, so I'd have to hack on the fly. I shrugged in response.

"More of a challenge for me, then. I'll see if I can leave his key card on the floor or something." Coach pulled me into an awkward half hug. "Stay as safe as you can. Okay?"

I nodded. "You too."

There were so many ways for this to go wrong.

He released me and gave one final nod before he pushed open the door. I watched the monitor as he approached the guard....

He strode right up to the guard as if he had a purpose, and they talked rather animatedly. The longer they talked the more anxious I became, even though the guard didn't look suspicious at all. Maybe it helped Coach was dressed in dark clothes, similar to the guard. I wasn't dressed for the part in blue jeans, hoodie, and backpack. I'd left all my black clothes at home.

Another clank from the door on the first floor.

Shit.

I couldn't leave this door. I'd need to get in fast if Coach cleared the way. Unless this person went to the basement, they would see me. There's no way I'd convince them I belonged here.

Someone moved light and fast on the stairs.

Coach continued to talk.

I couldn't enter the floor yet.

Backing up four steps into the shadows should keep me out of sight—unless they were going up to three.

I gasped as the person pushed on the bar to go through the door.

"Theo?" Eddie asked, looking right at me.

THIRTEEN

ANGRY. Freaked out. Sad. Relieved.

All those feelings jumbled together.

Just one would've been too much, but the combination threatened to short-circuit me.

Pain throbbed behind my eyes as a result.

"You came for Mitch." Eddie wasn't asking.

He knew.

He knew because he knew me.

He'd changed since I'd seen him last. Gone was the poufy Afro, and in its place, he had a very short cut that looked really good. He'd switched to contacts too. I knew from having tried on his glasses that they'd been real. He'd never have been able to stand wearing them otherwise....

As we stared at each other, I wanted to hug *and* punch him.

So many questions. Had he always been this close to home? Why turn up now? What would he do now that he'd discovered me?

I needed to get to Mitch and make sure he got out.

Instead, the person who ripped out my heart stood in

front of me, and I couldn't stop looking at how he'd changed.

The job needed my attention.

But he looked good. He was less lean and more muscular, meaning he likely wasn't swimming much. Even in the low light, the tight black long-sleeve shirt he wore couldn't conceal the ripples of muscle in his arms that weren't there before.

He raised an eyebrow—the usual move when he was waiting on me.

"Yeah," I finally answered. "He shouldn't be mixed up in this. I can't believe you went after Mitch and Iris." Fury at dragging our friends into this flared.

I came down the stairs and closed the space between us.

"That's why I'm here too." His voice didn't have the angry tinge mine did. "I heard that Mitch was brought in to force you to surrender. That was wrong." He looked away and down to the floor. "It's bad enough they came between us."

I grunted. I'd made sure never to involve Eddie in the TOS part of me. While I had no idea how I'd react if TOS had asked me to make a target out of him, I'd like to think I wouldn't have betrayed him.

"What was your plan to get him?" he asked.

"We're kind of flying by the seat of our pants."

"We?" That eyebrow went up again.

God, I missed him.

Breaching protocol, I showed him my phone where Coach continued chatting with the guard. I couldn't imagine what they were talking about all this time, but at least nothing bad was happening.

"Coach Daly too? How many of you guys were there?"

"I could ask you the same question."

"Right. Sorry."

I had a hard time reading him. That didn't use to be a problem.

"I'll take care of this," he said, moving for the door.

He produced two protein bars from his pants. They were chocolate mint—his favorite.

"Keep an eye on the screen, and once I'm in the room get yourself to the door."

He was through the door before I could say anything.

Insane.

How was I supposed to trust him? Who was to say he wouldn't betray Mitch?

Eddie strode down the hallway with the same confident walk I'd seen hundreds of times at school. It was disconcerting.

He walked right up to Coach and the guard. If Coach was shocked, I couldn't see it.

Eddie showed the bars and said something that made the guard and Coach walk away. Eddie watched for a moment and because I looked at the one screen, I couldn't see where they went. After a few beats, he turned and looked directly into the camera before swiping a key card and going inside.

So far he'd done exactly what he said he would. Without a moment's pause, I emerged from the stairwell, went quickly to the room, and through the door Eddie'd left ajar.

"...you do that to him? How are you even here?"

Eddie was on the floor with Mitch on top throwing punches as Eddie kept his head covered. I'd never seen Mitch like this, not even in the most physical games.

The door closed behind me, and I quickly tapped on the phone to force this room's feed to a freeze frame of Mitch that I'd captured earlier. It wasn't perfect by a long shot, but hopefully it would hold off from anyone coming to look.

"Mitch, stop. This isn't the time."

He stopped and looked my direction.

"Theo. Oh my God. How are you here?"

He scrambled off Eddie and threw himself around me. We held each other tight. He vibrated in my arms. I couldn't tell if it was anger, fear, or both.

"Theo, what's happening?"

"The less you know, the better," Eddie said.

Mitch clapped my back and stepped away. "I wasn't asking you." He whirled around and tensed up so fast I thought he might attack Eddie again. "I don't need to hear anything you have to say. You nearly destroyed Theo."

The door beeped, a green light flashing on the panel. Eddie stepped away before it opened. Coach slipped inside.

Mitch looked even more confused. I worried that he might shut down from shock.

"Coach?"

"Mitch." He nodded and then turned to Eddie. "I have no idea why you're here, but that was a good save. Thanks."

Eddie finally relaxed a little. Maybe he thought Coach was going to go after him too.

"I'm so confused," Mitch wavered, and I caught him before his legs gave out.

"Take it easy, man," I said, keeping him steady. "We're here to rescue you."

Mitch looked at me like I'd lost my marbles. "Be straight with me. Why am I here?"

I looked between Coach and Mitch. Coach eventually shrugged, which didn't help me out at all.

"Eddie's right. The less you know the safer you'll be." I

decided on as much truth as he'd get later. "The people who took you did it to get to me."

"It doesn't make sense. You know that, right?" Many times I'd wished I could get back to that state that Mitch lived—a place where teenagers didn't do the things Eddie and I did.

"No, it doesn't. But it's true. We need to get you out—now." I turned my attention to Coach. "How do we want to do this?"

"The plan was to go back the way we came. Is that good?" Coach looked to Eddie.

"Depends on how you got here."

We related how we got in, and Mitch stared at us while we talked. If this wasn't such a dangerous situation, I would've been amused by his look as he tried to process everything.

"That's probably best. You're not going out the front door even if I went with you. No one knows, unless they're actually watching the cameras, that I'm in here."

If they were watching the cameras?

"Stole my dad's key card," Eddie continued, holding it up. "I hadn't perfected how I was getting us out. You solved that problem." He looked a Coach.

"You expect me to jump between buildings?" Mitch asked, sounding alarmed.

"I did it," I said. "It's not that far."

Mitch threw his hands up and paced across the room and back. I felt bad. This kind of agitation was so far from his norm.

"Come on, Mitch," Coach said. "We need to go." Coach put his hand on Mitch's shoulder, and guided him toward the door. "In the hall we go to the left. The staircase is at the end of the hall and then up to the roof. I'll keep my hand on your shoulder so we stay close."

Just as Mitch was about to walk out, he looked to me and frowned. "Wait." He shrugged out of Coach's grip and came back inside. "What about you?"

Coach pulled Mitch back toward him.

"I'm not going," I said trying to sound confident in the decision. "They wanted me to come here—"

"You're okay with this?" Mitch looked back to Coach.

He nodded without hesitation.

"How can you stay here? We should call the police or… something."

"I've got no choice." Out of the corner of my eye I caught Eddie's concerned look as if he didn't like the plan. Would *he* let me walk out of here? Would he come with us?

"We really need to go," Coach said. "That guard is only gonna stay out so long."

"Go," I said. "I'll be fine."

"I wish I could believe that," Mitch said, his voice cracking.

I went and drew him into another hug. "This isn't my first time," I said, hoping to sell him on it. "I'll be fine." I tried to add more convincing emphasis.

We held each other's gaze, and I thought Mitch was going to argue more, but his look softened. "Take care of yourself, Theo."

"I'll do my best. I promise."

I held out my fist, he bumped it, and we traded weak smiles. He allowed Coach to take him out, but he stared at me until the door shut.

FOURTEEN

I watched the security feed as Coach and Mitch quickly got to the stairway and went up. As long as they weren't apprehended on the roof, they were safe.

"I'm surprised you didn't let Mitch wale on me," Eddie said when I'd pocketed the phone.

I took a breath and turned to fully face Eddie. While he sounded easygoing, his shoulders were tense. Shouldn't I be the tense one here?

The bright overhead fluorescent light made him look terrible as his dark skin took on a slightly yellowish tone. His eyes had no spark, no energy. I recognized the look— although it used to only surface when he had too many exams in a week.

Punch him or hug him? The battle raged on.

"There wasn't time for that."

He nodded. "Why didn't you go too?"

"You'd just come after me again. And who knows who you'd hurt the next time."

He flinched.

"It's not like I'm the one who captured him." His voice was low and frustrated. "Don't I get some credit for showing up to get him out?"

"And now he's gone, so why are you still here? Shouldn't you go before someone figures out you helped him?" I barely contained yelling at him, keeping my words clipped. In an effort to keep my simmering anger contained, I kept flexing my right hand into a fist.

"It's not like they won't figure it out when they see my dad's swipe on the door."

God, why couldn't I focus on being upset with him. The desire to close the space between us was intense.

"So what now? You get to finally turn me in?" The question wasn't really fair. If I could force him to stop being so earnest, maybe my frustration could fully take over, and I'd stop wanting to kiss him.

Eddie threw his hands up and made an exasperated sound. "Jesus, Theo. You think I like this? You're my boyfriend and—"

"I *was* your boyfriend. You don't get to call me that after what you did."

He looked around the room before finally turning away from me. With no windows and little furniture in the room, there wasn't much else to look at, though. "I had no choice. They threatened my mom. She has no idea what Dad's involved in and didn't deserve to get mixed up in it."

"And Mitch did?"

"You say that like I'm the one in charge." He stomped to the room's single chair, gripping the back while refusing to look at me. It looked like he fought the same anger I did. The muscles in his shoulders flexed along with his biceps.

He remained incredibly hot.

The fact that he could pick up the chair and swing at me didn't stop me from approaching.

"How long did you know?" I asked quietly. We needed to talk—maybe then I'd understand.

Releasing the chair, he turned with a defeated expression. "It wasn't too long after we got back from Denver." He shot a look up to the camera bubble on the ceiling.

"I'm feeding a still image for this camera. It may not be the best idea since they'll eventually notice and come investigate."

Eddie shrugged. "Depends on if the guy at the front desk is paying attention. More often than not he plays games on his phone. That's why I thought I could get Mitch out on my own."

So that's what he meant before.

"So you knew for, like, eight or nine months and never let on? Never told me I was in danger?"

"I didn't know what to do," he said, running a hand over his head. "It's not like I could tell somebody that my dad revealed he was some secret agent asking me to spy on my boyfriend. He said it would be worse for you if I didn't follow instructions. At first it was small stuff." His voice cracked a little as he talked. "Try to bug your phone. Try to put a trojan on your computer. Which, by the way, I said would never work because you were the security ace."

A smile crept across my lips. "Yeah, that was a fail." I smirked at him, feeling a few tendrils of our old energy coming back.

"Anyway, when you ended up working at Glenwood, they were already talking about sending me up to surprise you. When Sofia made the invitation, it became the perfect scenario." He rubbed his eyes, and I thought he might cry. "I don't know how you stay cool doing this stuff. It was the hardest thing in the world to get through dinner with you and wait for the drug to kick in."

The more he explained, the sadder he looked and the more my heart said to comfort him. I fought the ingrained reflexes to reach out, hold his hand, rub his back, or pull him close. He was part of why we were in this situation.

"Were you supposed to capture me that night? Melissa said—"

"I got in so much trouble." He winced. "I was supposed to leave the door unlocked when I left so they could take you. They wanted your parents asleep, and they planned to distract the guard. I couldn't allow it to happen. I locked the door and, since I was staying in the house, I set the alarm since the Glenwoods told me how to do that." He shrugged and looked back at the floor. "That blew their timeline. I couldn't let them take you."

We stood silent for way longer than we should've. His gaze finally drifted back up, and he looked so vulnerable. It reminded me of the looks he'd give me on some of our first dates—back when we fumbled kisses, tentatively touching each other when we went beyond kissing, and the first time we'd said "I love you."

My heart ripped into shreds.

Forced?

What could I do with that information? What would I have done if TOS asked me to do something against Eddie?

Eddie took a couple steps forward and instinctually I moved back. The hurt that crossed his face hurt my soul, but despite helping with Mitch, I couldn't trust him.

He stopped but kept his focus on me. "Can't I touch you?" The pleading in his voice didn't help my resolve. "Please? The way we said goodbye was—"

"The way you left things was fucked-up. There was no *we*."

"And I'll regret that forever. Nothing's been right since then. I had to protect Mom. I can't even see her. He took me away after I... I did what I did. Blackbird thought I was the key to getting you on board. Dad sold them on that, and he's made his disappointment clear that I failed. I think he keeps me close so I don't try to warn you. Of course, that doesn't matter now."

I had no words. If he was telling the truth, he was a pawn, which sucked.

"Level with me, Theo. Did you want this life? Would you have ever told me? Or would I have always been in the dark until you needed to use me like my Dad did?"

His body tensed, and I thought again he might lash out. At this point I had nothing to lose, so I told the truth.

"I've been in this since I was eleven. Denver was the first time I was in the field. I hated the secrets I had to keep. Not so much missions specifically, but that I couldn't tell you cool things I did or talk to you when things got difficult. I always had to hold back. It's supposed to help keep you, my friends safe—"

The catharsis of telling him just that little proved more powerful than I expected. I dabbed at my eyes before they overflowed. In the moment of vulnerability, Eddie closed the gap between us and drew me into a hug. He did what I couldn't during his confession.

I hugged him back—tight.

The rush of relief from touching him was strong. I hadn't realized how much I wanted it. I was scared to breathe for fear he'd disappear.

Eventually, I pulled back just enough to look up into his sad brown eyes. "Could I have done what you did? I don't know. If my mom was threatened… I'd like to think I'd have found another way, but…."

I hated the answer and tried to back out of the hug, ashamed.

He wouldn't let go. "Not yet."

I laid my head back against his shoulder as we kept a tight hold on each other. He'd definitely worked out more. I knew his body, and he had much more muscle.

"What do we do now?" I asked after some time had passed. I didn't let go to check my watch, but the deadline had to have passed.

"I don't know. We—"

The door lock clicked, and the door burst open. Two guards entered, guns drawn, followed by Westside and Eddie's father.

"What do you think you're doing, Relay?" Westside said. "Where's the kid?"

Relay? Was that Eddie's codename? Had he chosen a sports name? Did he know mine when he did it?

And kid. That was funny that they considered Mitch a kid when he was the same age we were.

Eddie didn't release me, so I couldn't fully face them.

"You got what you wanted," Eddie said flatly. "Mitch is gone. He's got nothing to do with this."

"You need to go wait in my office," Mr. Cochrane said, his eyes shooting daggers.

"No, he's a traitor now," Westside said. "Take these two to confinement. Make sure they have no electronics, especially Winger."

"But—" Mr. Cochrane said.

"No!" Westside remained shockingly firm. "We can't let Relay's feelings get in the way." He looked to the two guards again. "Take them."

Eddie and I released our hold before the guards got to us. We went silently.

Westside grabbed my arm to stop me before I got out of the room. "You and I have much to talk about."

FIFTEEN

Westside had seemed like a short-tempered, easily provoked, junior tech in Denver; yet he seemed to be running the show here.

Eddie had been stoic as a woman took him out of the room. I'd hoped to see where they put him, but Westside decided we'd talk first. "Since you're here, I'm not going after any more of your friends. But you need to follow instructions, or I'll get Mitch back. I'll get Iris, your teammates, whoever it takes."

He grabbed the phone out of my hand and jammed his hand into the pocket that held the unregistered one while a man held my arms behind my back. I didn't have the leverage or the strength to break the hold.

"Let's see what else you've got." He pulled my left arm toward him and pushed up the hoodie sleeve. He hastily jerked at the watchband until it released, and he took that as well. "I like that you came prepared. Take the pack off him."

The guard had surprising strength as he wrestled the backpack off my shoulders. I gave him no resistance, though.

I glared as he took my stuff.

"Take him to the basement. I'll send for you later."

We took the elevator down. Is this where Eddie was? For that matter, were there any TOS agents down here? Westside had made it sound like agents had been apprehended.

Considering what Westside said about Mitch, I had to assume that he and Coach got away. The mention of recapturing him sent chills through me. I hoped I wouldn't have to make a difficult choice—if they wanted me to do something detrimental to hundreds or thousands or millions of people, there'd have to be sacrifices.

Cinder blocks lined the hall. There were cameras in the ceiling, but this area wasn't on the set of cameras I'd viewed. Were these fake or had I missed a second system?

There were four steel, windowless doors on either side of the hall. The guard used his key card to open a door on the far end of the hall. To his credit he didn't shove me inside. Instead he let me go in before he shut the door.

The lighting came from four fluorescent bulbs in the ceiling, just like the room upstairs. A simple metal folding chair and standard, utilitarian folding table sat against one wall. There was a basic cot with a rumpled, thin mattress and small, sad pillow on the wall opposite the table. Electric outlets were on each wall. The ethernet outlet above the table surprised me. Not only did this seem like a dank place to work, but why put me in a room with that access—although I had nothing to plug into the port. In the middle of the ceiling, a camera stood watch. This would be a fisheye that covered the entire room. There'd be no privacy except for the three-quarter walled off area that had to be a bathroom. What I couldn't determine was if the room was mic'd. The safe assumption would be that someone listened to everything I might say.

As I finished inventory, I didn't know what I hoped to accomplish with the information. While I still wore the contact lenses—which would continue to function as long as the phone was within range and powered—they didn't have any major functionality to make use of. With the TOS network compromised, and only two other pairs of lenses out there, it wasn't like I could easily reach other agents to let them know where I was.

Putting the lenses to use, I found that the energy flow in the room wasn't surprising. The data looked normal too—in and out of the ethernet, the camera, and card lock. The other rooms on this floor seemed to have similar connections. At the door, I examined the card reader. It was metal and appeared to have no visible way in. I wouldn't be cracking it open.

Heat vision, which worked much better in here, registered two other people on the floor. The signature walking the hall had to be the guard. The other was sitting and must be in a room like I was.

Eddie?

Eddie's allegiances confused me. He put up no fight over being taken into custody and his father's disappointment didn't faze him. Was he an ally or pretending?

He said he'd shown up to free Mitch, but part of me wondered if they sent him in to ensure that I'd stay.

I dropped into the chair behind the table.

And what did Westside want from me? The thought of our talk yet to come made my heart thump faster and spread anxiety through my chest. Nothing he'd want could be good.

Being at the source of the problem was oddly comforting, definitely better than being on the outside trying to figure out what to do. Confinement in Denver had freaked me out, but I didn't feel that way—at least not yet.

These lenses required a new function—ability to control the phone. That would be incredibly helpful in situations like this. It shouldn't even be that hard to set up given the connection that was already established between the devices.

A chuckle escaped. Sometimes my mind worked in bizarre ways—how could I come up with a lens enhancement while imprisoned? It was a pretty big leap to think that I'd be working on the lenses again anytime soon.

The bolt on the door popped, and while the noise startled me, I put my composure in place before the door opened. Plus, the less I reacted the better.

Westside entered with the guard who'd brought me here.

"I'm sure you checked everything out and found that there's no way for you to escape from this room." He looked at me as the guard closed the door behind them. They made no move toward me. The guard stood against the door, and Westside was about two paces in front of him.

I said nothing.

"Have I broken you already? You had so much more bluster last time." He paused but continued when I stayed quiet. "Why don't we go somewhere a little more comfortable," Westside said. "You've had a hectic twenty-four hours. Let's relax over dinner?"

What made him think I could relax? I'd be tense until he paid for what he'd done.

The guard swiped his key, opened the door, and stepped aside. I still didn't get up.

"Come on." He gestured to the door. "We need to talk about how you'll help us. The sooner we get this done, the better for everyone."

I relented. I had to know what terrible thing he wanted to figure out how to stop it.

SIXTEEN

WESTSIDE SWIPED his key card at the door farthest from the elevator on the third floor. The room easily took up a third—if not half—of the floor. It opened into a comfortable office that any tech company CEO might have. A bunch of monitors filled a wall adjacent to windows that looked out over the street. A sleek steel desk with a chair, and a large desktop monitor, sat in front of two guest chairs. A couch faced the monitor wall. In the opposite corner a circular table surrounded by six chairs had two place settings with metal domes over the plates. A slight smell of grilled beef filled the room.

An embarrassingly loud growl came from my stomach. It'd been several hours since I'd had anything to eat, and my stomach wasted no time calling dibs on whatever was under the dome.

"I figured you'd be hungry, so dinner seemed appropriate while we talked."

Who was this nice guy?

The guard stepped back outside and didn't seem to lock the door—at least no sound alerted that a bolt had snapped in place. The camera in the ceiling, just like the one in the room I'd been in, made it clear Westside had backup if he needed it.

Despite my stomach I held my ground and stayed just inside the door. Westside removed the plate covers to reveal hamburgers and fries. An interesting choice since it mirrored the last meal Eddie and I had shared. Was it deliberate or a coincidence?

My stomach rumbled again, even louder—not helping. It hadn't been that long since I'd eaten, had it? Sometime this morning, I think.

"Go ahead, have a seat." He gestured to one of the chairs as he went to a fridge built into the monitor wall. He pulled out two sodas. "Dr Pepper, as I recall, for you?"

I stared at him.

"Let's not play—"

"After what you had Eddie do to me, do you really think I'd eat with you?"

He nodded twice and smiled. "That's reasonable. Look, you're already here. If it makes you feel better, you can get your own drink. You'll find that they're all sealed up and haven't been tampered with. You can decide which burger you want too. They're the same, both cooked medium."

Pissing him off would accomplish nothing.

"Fair enough." I went to the fridge and removed a bottle of Dr Pepper. It was sealed as it made the satisfying snap of the plastic cap releasing from the ring. I examined the bottle and didn't see any patched pinholes. As a last check, I put the cap back on and turned the bottle over to see if there were any leaks above the fluid line or in the cap. It seemed okay.

"Cautious, methodical. Nicely done."

The compliment bugged me. All I wanted from him were answers.

"Now please, have a seat so we can eat before this gets cold."

He went to the table and stood, waiting for me to make my choice. He stood at the midpoint of the table. Ultimately, I chose the chair closest to me, set my soda on the table, and dropped into the chair.

My stomach rumbled yet again.

"Please, eat. There'll be time to talk afterward."

He picked up his burger and took a bite as he kept his eyes focused on me. There might be a rule that I'd learn one day about not eating with the enemy, but right now it seemed like the right thing. I needed to keep my strength up and, according to my stomach, I wasn't doing a good job.

Mom would've been proud as I kept my manners in check—even placing the napkin in my lap before I took my first bite.

It was good. Wherever he'd gotten this from, knew how to make a good burger. I managed to not wolf too much of it down at once.

"Good, right?

"It is. Thank you."

He nodded. "See, we can be friends."

"Friends don't exactly do the kind of things you've done."

Surreal.

That was the only word that came to mind.

Having dinner and a civilized conversation with a guy who I would just as soon punch was bizarre.

Truthfully, I'd rather do much more than a single hit, even though violence isn't my go-to. He deserved it. And I hoped I got the chance....

No!

The voice in my head spoke loud and clear.

I couldn't think like that. It wouldn't make this situation better. And I really didn't want to stoop to his level. I'd defend myself if needed and would do my best to not get provoked into more. John would expect me to keep my cool as much as possible in this situation.

Once Westside got halfway through his burger, he took a drink and even wiped his mouth before speaking.

"All right. Let me tell you what's happened. We have total control of the TOS network. With the tracking system, we've captured or killed 85 percent of the agents." I flinched, and I hated that I did it. "I assure you that we've only killed those who put up a fight or posed a threat to Project Override. For the people that want to work with us, we're allowing them to under supervision. The rest we're holding until we complete Override."

There were thousands of agents—even I didn't know the exact number despite the fact I created tech to support everyone. It seemed impossible they could get that many.

"As for your parents," he said, almost sounding sad, "your mother was having none of it and put up a fight that she lost. Your father is unaccounted for, somewhere in Europe. It doesn't matter. He can finish whatever it is he's doing, and we'll intercept him when he returns to the States. We have Lorenzo Davenport in custody. His knowledge is too valuable to kill him, but eventually his usefulness will run out for us if he doesn't start cooperating more."

I swallowed hard. He looked serious, but it could be a game. It'd better be a lie because I couldn't imagine the alternative.

Dad was in Europe when I'd checked a few hours back. But Mom appeared to be in Canada. She wouldn't let herself get killed. They likely did have Lorenzo, though, based on what I'd seen.

What I wouldn't do was give this man the satisfaction of seeing more of a reaction than I'd already let slip.

"They've been training you," he said after a few moments of silence where I kept eating fries. "You couldn't keep your mouth shut last time we met. Shadowcaster told me you seemed more thoughtful."

Shadowcaster had to have been Melissa, the Blackbird agent who'd been undercover at Glenwood Music. The woman who'd also identified herself as Westside's wife.

"So tell me about Override?" I finally asked.

I didn't need his commentary. My focus revolved around his plans and the part he needed me to play.

A smile played across his lips. The urge to wipe it off surged through me.

"In due time. A few more things need to click into place before I put you to work. That should be done by morning. I dug into your background once I escaped from TOS and built up a significant dossier on you. I shouldn't have underestimated you before. Imagine my surprise at the beautiful coincidence that one of our top agents happened to be your boyfriend's father. Almost Shakespearean in some ways."

That landed like a gut punch and for a moment I thought I might lose the burger.

John loved Shakespeare. He'd studied literature extensively and always loved a good book. He tried to pass on his passion to me. Sometimes I got it and sometimes I didn't. He considered it a success when he got me to appreciate—and even admit to liking—*Ragtime* last year, which I'd struggled with as one of my American lit assignments.

I wiped my mouth and tried to take some calming breaths. Hopefully I hid the pangs of sadness.

"Two families against each other," Westside continued, looking pleased with himself. "Nonetheless, this isn't going to be a monologue. While I don't think you could prevent any part of the plan, there's no need to give you time to think more about it. You might as well finish dinner, and then you can get a good night's sleep."

Dammit. I really wanted the movie-like reveal.

"What have you done with Eddie? You can't be happy he chose me in the long run."

"Did he?" Westside smirked.

Based on how he was taken out of the room it seemed obvious that he had chosen. Or did I see what I wanted to? Of course, it could be a tactic too, just like what he told me about Mom.

I ate the rest of the food, even though I rapidly lost my appetite.

SEVENTEEN

I LAY ON THE BED, hoping to get some rest. That burger had landed in my stomach like a brick. Had I picked the wrong plate?

The conversation with Westside replayed on a loop in my brain as I desperately looked for clues. Override meant nothing to me. If TOS knew of that project, the info hadn't made it to me. The more I considered dinner, it seemed he delighted in toying with me, maybe beating me down a little. Could I believe anything he said?

I thought myself into a headache—my right temple throbbing.

Westside talked like he needed me. Surely, he wouldn't take me out with food.

Without my watch I had no idea how long it had been since dinner. I figured it'd been two or three hours.

The bolt on the door clicked.

I looked over, but the door didn't open.

I counted to sixty and nothing happened.

Slowly I crossed the room. While I might be on camera, I couldn't pass up the chance to do some reconnaissance.

I slipped into the hallway and closed the door behind me. If there was an alarm system and the lock reengaged, the door needed to be closed. If I got caught, so be it.

The guard had taser leads sticking out of his chest that left him unconscious on the floor. I'd heard nothing from inside the room. I flicked the contacts over to heat and the other cell was empty, no sign of the other person from earlier. Had all the locks opened? Could Eddie have been put down here?

"Theo." I looked to the end of the hall, and Eddie peeked out from the stairwell door. I ran for the door, and he opened it farther so I could slip into the low-light space. We ended up pressed together, and I wished my body wouldn't react to his proximity. I didn't need the rush of feelings—this wasn't the time to deal with any of that.

Westside's question reverberated through my head too.

"What are you doing?" I asked, putting a bit of distance between us.

"We need to get out of here and put a stop to what's happening."

"How do I know I can trust you?" Frustration filled my voice. "Do you even know what Override is?"

"We're only safe for a few minutes. I forced a reboot on the security system."

That sounded like something I'd try, but I wouldn't have expected Eddie to know how. I'd always been his tech support before.

"How are you even—"

"Dad was pissed Westside hauled me away, and he somehow got me released. He didn't know I've been stealing his passwords. He uses the same few for everything, so it was easy to break into his computer and use his credentials to reset the system. Now come on. We can't let them get away with what they're trying to do."

He'd managed to pull off a useful distraction. Although it might not have been the best time to do it.

"I still don't know what the plan is. I can't stop what I don't know."

"It's not about you stopping it. I'm talking about the FBI or CIA or something."

"You've no idea who to trust. If you go to those places, you could end up talking to somebody who is Blackbird. TOS had people inside many agencies."

He looked frustrated, and I couldn't blame him. We were spending too much time standing around. How long was it going to take for the system to reboot? And what if they sent somebody specifically to check on me?

"Westside seems to think he needs me to finish Override. If I walk away, they'll just go after Mitch or someone again."

Eddie sighed.

Maybe he hadn't thought through everything. I certainly hadn't.

"Look, if I take you to where the main computers are could you wipe them out?"

"Probably. Might take some time depending on the security involved."

Eddie ran his hand over his head and looked like he might actually freak out. Whatever he knew he really didn't like it.

"Tell me. We can figure out a plan." I took his hand, hoping to calm him. "I have no doubt we can stop, or at least put a significant dent in the plan. I just need to know what it is."

"They want to take full control of the internet. They've caused outages on and off over the past couple of days. They want to charge companies and governments to keep it operating. Can you imagine how messed-up everything will be?"

Could they have really come up with a reasonable way to control the entire internet? I could understand taking out parts of it, but there were so many redundancies built in over the years to prevent outages, it didn't seem possible. If they could do that, shockwaves would go through every aspect of the economy and life as we knew it.

My understanding about the inner workings of the internet came from MIT and what I knew from TOS and how it used the net to monitor agents and network tech. Shutting the whole thing down or even controlling vast parts of it seemed impossible. Blackbird would've had to come up with some impressive tech for that to work.

"Care to share what you're thinking?" Eddie asked, snapping me back to the conversation. "I recognize that face."

I couldn't hold back a smile. "Sorry. Just working through the ramifications. I guess after years of trying to destabilize individual parts of the world and pockets of commerce, they'd try to go for something big."

"We need to go." Eddie looked jittery. "We need help. Unless you think you can stop this."

"Same problem as before. I don't know if I can stop it since I don't know how they're doing it. I've seen a couple of internet issues today. Obviously, those were Blackbird. But they seemed random and not something on the level that they're trying to do. Maybe it's not perfected yet."

"Could that be why they want you?"

I was good at what I did. But taking over the net was beyond my skills. "You think we can get to my phone and computer?"

Eddie shook his head. "That's risky. I assume it's in Westside's office."

"What are our options? You know this place better than I do."

Just like he recognized my thinking face, I recognized his.

"It's late so there aren't many people around," he said. "He's probably gone. But this seems like a really bad idea. Can't we just go?"

"No. I need that stuff."

"Does it have to be this hard?"

"You'd be amazed." I grinned, and he raised an eyebrow. Nothing was ever as easy as it should be. "Let's go."

I took the steps two by two, and he kept pace right behind me. Before we got to the third floor my breath came in gasps. I shouldn't be winded from that short burst.

The third floor was quiet.

Before we were halfway to Westside's office, the loud snap of all the locks on the floor startled me.

"We're outta time," Eddie had a quiver of fear in his voice.

"We've got to go back downstairs."

"What?" he asked in a shockingly loud voice.

"I can't leave. You know that." I grabbed his hand and pulled on him to head back to the stairs. "And it'll get bad for both of us if we're caught out here."

"Fine." He moved into resignation. "I've got a keycard, so I can get you back in."

So much for getting my stuff.

We took off, which wasn't easy. I shouldn't be this slug-gish. Even if dinner didn't sit well, it was still protein and energy."

EIGHTEEN

I DIDN'T WANT to wake up. If I didn't open my eyes, maybe I could go back to sleep.

The dreams had been so good—hanging out with Eddie, playing hockey, and going to Disney World with my family, John, Eddie, and Henrik Zetterberg.

The dream made no sense. Especially hanging out with Zetterberg, who was super friendly and beyond cute in shorts and a Mickey Mouse tank top. He made sure we had Fast Passes for everything.

Also odd was that we'd never been to Disney. We'd thought about it a couple years ago, but we'd gone up to Maine and rented a cabin for a month the summer between my freshman and sophomore years. I'd freaked the first few days because there was no service up there, but then I kind of liked it—though I didn't want to admit it. John came up for a week too. It'd been fun. I hadn't been that unplugged and....

John.

We should've done more trips like that.

How did I just leave him on the floor?

Run.

His words echoed loudly.

I shuddered and then coughed. It felt like sandpaper in my mouth.

"Oh my God. You're awake." A chair scraped across the floor. As I focused Eddie came to me.

I fluttered open my eyes. Eddie?

It felt like I hadn't moved in days, my muscles far tighter than expected. I knew I had been tired, but this was ridiculous.

What'd happened?

For a moment it was like waiting for a video to buffer with pixilation and choppy sound. The memory eventually cleared up—forcing out the dream.

The system had rebooted. We scrambled back down here and....

I had no idea.

Eddie parked himself on the very edge of the twin bed.

"You kinda got sick." He must've seen my confusion. "Coming back downstairs you almost passed out, but I caught you." He smiled a bit. "I'm back in lockdown because I tried to help you escape, but they don't know how far we actually got. They know I hacked the security system and tasered the guard, but they don't know we were upstairs. I told them I found you sick."

How did this keep getting worse? I should've stayed in Disney World.

At least I knew why I'd felt weird after dinner.

"Am I okay?" I croaked out, shocked at how bad I sounded.

"Just a sec. Let me get you some water."

He brought the chair over with a cup of water and straw.

"How long was I out?"

He positioned the cup and straw, so I could drink. It tasted good, so good. But I made sure to take it slow.

"That's better. Thanks." I sounded more like myself now. I tried to sit up, but Eddie put a hand firmly on my chest before I got too far.

"Stay put. You've been out for about thirty-six hours. The doctor wants you to rest until she comes back tonight."

I nodded and relaxed a bit. I could.

"So, anyway, the doctor said you were super dehydrated not to mention exhausted. They've been running IV fluids to get you fixed up. Of course, the sleep has been good for you too. Westside was convinced you tried to poison yourself to get out of this."

I softly chuckled at the idea that I'd get sick on purpose. "Does that mean I get a doctor's note, so I can go home?"

Eddie ran his hand through my hair, pushing some of it back from my forehead. It was a loving touch, one he'd done many times before. A sigh escaped before I could stop it.

"The best you'll get is another day to rest."

If Eddie heard the sigh, he didn't respond to it. He continued stroking my hair, though, and a lump formed in my throat because of how it comforted me. Not only was it something he used to do when we were snuggled together but it reminded me of my mom because she always did this when I got sick. I probably shouldn't be thinking of my boyfriend—or former boyfriend—and my mom at the same time, but I couldn't help it.

"The doctor made it clear that you need time for your body to recover. Westside griped that he expected better from an athlete, but she did a great job putting him in his place. I'm not sure if he was serious about someone making sure you drank enough once you were on your feet, but he did mention it."

I sucked at this being on the run business.

At least I could use the recuperation time to consider my next step.

"How'd I end up with you watching over me?" I took one hand out from under the sheet and held his free hand.

"They decided someone should be in here full-time since the camera might not catch you getting worse. Since they were going to lock me up anyway, they decided it might as well be in here." He dropped his hand from my head down to my chest, laying it across my heart. "You worried me. Sometimes you were babbling in your sleep—funnel cakes and Space Mountain. It made no sense. Anyway, you need to be more careful."

Oh jeez.

I winced wondering what else I might have said.

"I thought I was just extra tired," I said, ignoring the Disney references. "I didn't know how bad it was until it was too late. You'd think I'd know better, even with all this crazy, to not let myself get so dried out."

He offered a slight smile, and I returned it. In that moment, it felt like no time had passed. I loved him despite what he'd done, and being around him only amplified it, even if getting back with him might not be the best thing for me.

"Anyway, thank you. I can't think of anyone else I'd rather have taking care of me." That was the truth.

He leaned down and put a kiss on my cheek.

My stomach spoke up, breaking the moment. I hadn't gotten too embarrassed before over the babbling, but my hunger growl caused the heat to rise in my face.

"Any chance I get some soup, maybe?"

Eddie got up and went to the door. "Chicken noodle or some of that nasty tomato stuff you like?"

The gleam in his eye was so familiar. I couldn't let him woo me. Not when there were so many things at stake.

"I'll go with the chicken noodle."

He rapped on the door, and it opened. No one entered, but he reported that I was awake, coherent, and wanted food.

Eddie resumed his position in the chair and held my hand, which I squeezed.

This was so wrong. He'd sold me out, and I kept doing stupid things like holding his hand as if nothing had happened. Should I forgive that? My heart fluttered. Maybe we could mend us.

"You thinking about how to fix all this?"

He read me way too well, which was probably part of the problem. "I should be thinking about Override. Instead" —I held up our interlocked fingers—"I'm thinking about this."

He tried to pull back, but I wouldn't let him go.

"You're kinda giving mixed messages."

"Yeah, well, welcome to my confusion. What are we supposed to do about us?"

"Don't you think we should figure out how to deal with the worldwide problem first?"

"Yeah, but the fact you're here makes me wonder if Westside's using you to keep a close eye on me. It looks like you're trying to help...." I really didn't know what else to say to him. I laid my cards on the table. He relaxed his hand as I held it.

He nodded but didn't look upset. "I messed up big, and I can't expect you to forgive me all at once." He kept his eyes on mine, not turning away for even a moment. "I'll do what I have to to prove that you can trust me again. I'm not going to be forced into hurting you again."

We stayed quiet for a moment as my hand flexed around his and his did the same in mine.

"Let's talk about something easier. Do I have clothes somewhere?"

He grinned mischievously. "Maybe I convinced everyone that you need to work in just your boxers." He darted his eyes between me and other points in the room—his typical embarrassed look. "I've missed that, you know, among all the other things I miss."

I shook my head and smirked. "After everything, this is what you thought about?" I used my free hand to move the covers aside, so he could see my bare chest and a bit of boxers.

He nodded slowly. He probably didn't know how perfect that response was. My pulse rose, and my heart got the fluttery feeling it always did when I got flirty with Eddie.

"The doctor had us strip you because you'd gotten really sweaty. They're in the bathroom to dry out."

Gross. Those were going to be less than fun to put back on.

"I asked them to get you some clothes since you're going to be here awhile. I knew you wouldn't want to wear those until they were washed."

Taking care of me like he always did. Another point in the "why Eddie should be trusted" column.

The door lock clicked, and it opened. Two women came in—one holding the door, standing guard, and another with a tray containing soup and Dr Pepper. My mouth watered as the chicken aroma wafted to me.

"There's more soup if you need it," the tray carrier said.

"We didn't know how much you'd eat. Westside wants to see you later this afternoon once you've got more strength. You'll have new clothes in the next hour too."

I nodded. No way could I say "thank you" to my captors.

Without a word they left. Once the door was closed, the sound of the lock clicking into place echoed through the room.

Eddie went to the desk and checked over the tray. This scene had played out a couple times in the past when one of us got sick. Last spring I'd brought him multiple vegetable beef servings from our favorite diner when his allergies got the better of him. Prior to that, he and John nearly drowned me in various assortments of soup when I'd gotten the cold from hell just after Thanksgiving.

That memory slammed me into a brick wall.

John was a trained agent, but he knew exactly how to take care of a kid. He got me through chicken pox when I was seven. I'd been a cranky, itchy patient but he made it better with all the right foods and a vat of lotion.

"You want it over there or do you want to eat here?" Eddie's question snapped me back before I got lost in the grief.

I sighed softly. Looking over at him as he waited for my answer, my heart somersaulted again. Figuring him out might be more difficult than stopping Override. "It'll do me good to get up, I think."

I ignored the fact that I was in only boxers. Luckily the room was a comfortable temperature, so I slowly got up as he took the soup bowls off the tray—they'd brought him some too. At the foot of the bed, I spotted my hoodie and tossed that on, though I didn't zip it.

For the first time in months, I got to have a meal with Eddie.

He'd done nothing here but help me. Yet, as I sat down, the thought that bounced around my head featured me waking up out of a paralysis. He'd drugged my soda. I wanted so much to trust and love him. My agent side flared —just as it had when I had dinner with Westside—with a warning to be vigilant.

No!

With so much of my world upside down, I wanted to enjoy the simplicity of eating with Eddie. If it turned into a mistake, I'd deal with it later.

NINETEEN

THE MORE I ate the more I wanted it. I usually ate on a regular schedule. One of the first things I'd learned in hockey was the importance of fueling the body right, and I'd taken that seriously for years.

It'd never occurred to me I could forget to drink enough water after years of being consistent. It was stupid I'd let something so simple sideline me.

The message icon flashed in my vision, and I coughed as I choked on the soup.

The phone's charge was lasting above and beyond expectation. It had a high-performance battery and the fact that it was still going, proved it'd been designed right. It helped that the phone wasn't doing much, but still —impressive.

"You okay?" Eddie looked ready to leap into action.

"Yeah, yeah. Just tried to inhale the soup, that's all."

While I wanted to trust him, he didn't need to know everything. He offered a weak smile, no doubt knowing I hid something. He kept one eye on me as he went back to his food.

I opened the message.

Winger? It's Locksmith.

No way. How could it be.

Locksmith, a.k.a. Dean Brody, was a hacker who was also a student last year at McKinley. He'd been in the computer science club and played a major role in stopping the sale of an encrypted key. We'd become something between acquaintances and friends after that. I had no idea how he'd accessed the lenses, much less how he knew my codename.

D-Man is here with me.

Whoa! How did Coach know to track him down?

I struggled to show no reaction despite the excitement and relief. It pained me a bit to hold back since I really wanted to celebrate like I'd scored a goal.

The connection to the outside meant help.

It took some time for me to type out a longer message, but I got it: *Dude. Cool. How? Can you share vid?*

I wasn't sure he could since there was no way he was on lenses himself, but if he was able to send a message, he might be able to do video.

Hold on.

Hopefully Coach had also made sure that Mitch was well protected.

A small window opened, and I saw Dean. I shared the lenses' view back to him.

You're with Eddie?

Of course that would be the thing that caught Dean's attention. I hadn't seen Dean since school started, but he knew Eddie and I had broken up.

Dean had transformed a little in the past few weeks. College seemed to agree with him—he looked more "preppy college student" than "grungy high schooler."

"What are you doing?" Eddie stared at me. I must've looked weird staring ahead and eye darting around.

I didn't answer. I might be willing to trust him, but I had to assume this room was mic'd. I shrugged. "What are you talking about?"

The confused look was endearing, and I imagined his brain grinding away trying to figure out what I didn't say. "I'm just gonna sit here and eat."

His smile grew into one I recognized from the old days when I went off on technospeak he didn't understand. He seemed to understand that something was happening, though.

I'd love a way to type like Lorenzo, and I had before. It seemed like forever to get a few short sentences out.

Yeah. He's helped. I got sick.

His response was much faster as he typed on a regular keyboard: *That explains why you didn't answer before. We'd left some messages, but when you didn't respond I'd erased them until I could make sure you'd see them while we were at the computer.*

While I typed a question about Mitch, Dean provided the answer—Mitch, Iris, and their families were under the protection of people Coach trusted. If he put his faith in them, that was all I needed to know.

So, Winger. And I have to say it's so cool you've got a secret agent name. Anyway, sorry, D-Man says you probably need help. What can I do?

Coach stepped in behind Dean. Seeing him provided another shot of relief. I had people on the outside, including someone who was very good with tech. It gave me true hope for the first time in a while.

Not sure. Blackbird trying to take internet. Need more details.

Since Coach was with Dean, I assumed it wasn't out of bounds reporting what I did. Dean wasn't TOS, but he was deputized, and I knew Coach would make sure he didn't tell anyone he shouldn't.

Coach slid a chair next to Dean and they talked for a second. I ate, since I had a break in typing. I raised my eyebrows at Eddie and smiled letting him know things were good.

If you have comms there's some limited operability and we might be able to get some audio from you.

Comms were close—but stuck in my backpack in Westside's office. If I saw a chance to get them, I'd try.

Can't get comms now.

Understood.

Coach pulled his phone and looked at the screen. He held up a finger and stepped out of frame. Was that good or bad?

I typed: *Thanks. Sorry to drag you in.*

Dean grinned and shrugged. Not exactly the reaction I expected. *Are you kidding. This is movie stuff. I know it's serious but come on. I'm talking to someone through a contact lens. Someone who's a freaking spy.*

I'd felt like that on missions before, especially when I was behind a keyboard. I couldn't find that same excitement in this scenario, but I couldn't fault Dean for it.

Coach stepped back into view, and he actually looked happy. He said something to Dean that made him get up so Coach could sit.

Coach typed: *I've got someone who wants to be seen.*

Lorenzo maybe? Maybe someone higher up at TOS?

He turned the phone screen to me.

My heart nearly pounded out of my chest, and I shook uncontrollably.

"Theo?" Eddie put his spoon down and reached for one of my hands. I shook so hard it shook his.

Dad's face filled the screen, and he looked okay in the black-and-white view. I couldn't see behind him so there was no way to know his location.

I wiped my eyes. Holding back the tears proved difficult, but I had to so I could see clearly.

Dad's mouth moved, and Coach typed.

"Theo?" Eddie asked.

"I'm fine," I croaked out. "I need a minute."

I struggled to read the text: *Defender is okay. Still on his mission. Trying to get back to the States but extracting himself is difficult. I updated him on your situation. He says he loves you. He knows you're going to be smart.*

Thank God. So many emotions swirled—almost more than I could manage. I exhaled hard. Eddie got up, came over, and pulled my head into his stomach in a sort of hug.

My breathing got ragged, and I fought against completely falling apart. Eddie both comforted me and blocked the surveillance camera. Despite the reunion happening in my eye, it wasn't lost on me that Eddie likely deliberately picked this exact spot to stand.

Love you too.

I usually made sure to keep to protocol, but so much had already gone out the window I didn't really care.

Dad nodded. Coach must be reading what I wrote to him. Dad then talked some more, and Coach typed.

Snowbird is fine. She's relocated and safe. She's worried about you, but I'll let her know we've talked.

Dad stepped back from his phone a bit and there was an unremarkable wall behind him. He put his hand up and made a fist and bumped it against the camera then pulled back just enough to lay his palm over the camera.

Our long-distance hug.

He left his palm there for a few seconds before he pulled back and gave me a thumbs-up.

It hurt not to scream as my body tensed wanting the release. This could be the last time I'd see him. I shuddered, and Eddie hugged me closer.

I typed as quick as I could: *Wait.*

They needed to see that, so Dad wouldn't hang up. I had more to say.

Eddie stepped back as I pushed away from him and the table. Without a word I went into the bathroom and looked into the mirror. I wanted Dad to see me—just in case.

My mouth dropped open. I looked horrible—a few days of stubble, eyes that showed how wiped I was, and hair all over the place. Dad had the same expression.

Coach typed: *What have they done to you? You look awful.*

His concerned look punched me in the chest.

I'm okay. Been sick. Better now. Back to work soon.

Dad nodded but still looked horrified.

I raised my palm to my eyes and held it close as a response to what Dad had done.

Be safe. Tell Snowbird I love her.

This was the most time-consuming communication ever. I waited for Coach to send the next message and looked into the mirror as if Dad was just on the other side.

D-man typed, and I eventually had a message back: *I love you Winger. I'll try to check in with D-Man or you tomorrow.*

Dad cried, and that was the end of holding mine in. Coach and Dean looked somber as Coach typed more.

I'm sorry I'm not there to help.

It's okay. I didn't know what else to say. He put his palm back on the screen, and I put mine in front of my face again. I held it until his screen went dark.

I gripped the sides of the sink and cried.

Need minute. I managed to type, and I cut the video feed.

Knowing Mom and Dad were alive and somewhat safe put me at ease and yet totally freaked me out. Dad's complete faith in me should've given me strength, but I felt all the more alone.

"Not sure what's up," Eddie said quietly. I looked up and saw him reflected in the mirror from where he stood in the doorway. "The guard came in and asked what was wrong because you bolted for the bathroom. I said maybe you'd eaten too fast."

"Thanks," I squeaked out.

Someone typed: *Standing by.*

He came in and held me.

I sobbed.

So much poured out, it scared me that it wouldn't stop. Eddie rubbed my back and held me tight. He knew what I needed, and he didn't hesitate, even though he didn't know what happened—and he didn't ask.

Eventually I calmed and had to pull back to get a tissue.

"Sorry," I said, looking at Eddie.

I typed back to the guys too: *Thanks for that.*

"Don't apologize. What's happened?"

It was time to trust him—in here were the camera couldn't see. "I've got a way to communicate," I said quietly, into his ear since I didn't know how sensitive any mics might be. "I found out Mom and Dad are okay. I... I need to get back to work."

The sooner I stopped Override, the sooner I could get back to normal.

"Are you sure you've rested enough?" I loved him for not questioning anything about how I got the information I did.

"It doesn't matter. There's a job to do."

What can we do? D-Man and I are still here.

Not sure. Typing was tough as I dried up the tears. *Need plan. Stand by.*

I have an alert set so if you send a message we'll know. We're here for whatever you need.

Dean was amazing. He dove right in with no idea what was to come. And then there was Eddie just rolling with what was happening—really like he always had.

"I'll see about your clothes," Eddie said.

I stopped him before he got to the door, catching him by the shoulder. "Thank you"—he turned back to me—"for taking care of me. And not asking too many questions."

"It's the least I can do." He brought his hand to mine, which was still on his shoulder. "You should take a shower. I know that'll make you feel better."

"For sure."

I got yet another smile before he left the bathroom. As soon as I cleaned up, I'd go see Westside, so I could get back to planning his downfall.

TWENTY

"We want controls in place, so we govern who has access to the internet at any given time. There's a lot of money and power to be had controlling how and when information can be passed. It used to be you needed gold or weapons for leverage. Today it's all about data. We've got most of the infrastructure and code in place and with your help we can finish."

Westside sounded completely sane as he laid out the bonkers plan.

"It's difficult to control something that's so huge and has the redundancies the internet has," he continued. "We've been working over the last week to test parts of our technology and we see that we don't have enough control in place. The only way the plan works is if the control is absolute."

Any kind of massive internet outage would cause so much chaos, which was exactly what Blackbird liked to do. As connected as the world was, such a disruption could even be deadly.

"I already see your trying to work through how you can

prevent this. I would hope you've seen how powerful we are between tearing apart TOS and abducting those close to you if we have to. There's quite a lot we can do to *you* as well. You were affected by our audio experiment, and I could try out the latest incarnation on you and see how that goes."

Dammit.

He had me, and he knew it. He'd seen the lengths I'd go to when I'd worked to rescue Dad in Denver and Mitch here.

Chills went down my spine as I considered how they could've expanded the audio program since we'd shut it down. I was confident they weren't broadcasting it over the internet, although if they got control of the internet, that could change. There were other ways they could use the audio tech as well.

"I don't even know how to do what you're talking about. Getting control over something as large as the internet would involve oversight and dominance over millions of individual hubs." I stopped. He didn't need more of my thoughts.

"We thought of all that. But you're right—the trick is executing it."

My head swam as I tried to comprehend the vastness of Override. Going against a system that was designed to be resilient was something you spent years on. And even then, the system itself would continue to evolve to be stronger. Denial of service attacks against a single entity or even a particular backbone of the internet was one thing, but this was far beyond that.

"There are governments that prevent their citizens from accessing certain things," Westside continued. "China routinely blocks websites. Egypt, Myanmar, and others have shut the net down at times. Remember the controversy over repealing net neutrality here because it would allow providers to block content or throttle speed? We're simply taking that to a new level."

"But you're talking about putting a control on top of everything else. It's one thing for a country to block sites, or even order a shutdown. But I just don't see...." This discussion was something we might tackle in a class as a theoretical exercise. It was hard to believe someone wanted to attempt it.

"That's why we need your help. We've got a lot of smart people here, and you're a great addition to the team. Let me show you." He opened his laptop, typed a few keys and a bunch of code and notes came up on the wall of screens. He got up from his desk and walked over. I followed.

"We've tested with varied success. We've disrupted credit card transactions, corporate interconnectivity, individual internet providers, and we had about ten hours where we had a major backbone down, causing a lot of issues on the West Coast. Sometimes our efforts were taken out by security measures, but usually we were able to complete our test. We need our own resiliency, though. You specialize in writing scripts and bots to carry out commands, and the team thinks that's exactly what we need—especially ones that can adapt so they can keep control."

That might be possible, but... I didn't see how anything that complex could be written, tested, and deployed quickly.

"What you see here," he continued while pointing to several screens of code, "are some of our attempts to create bots that can take instructions and adapt. We need better ones. Your ability to design bots is more advanced than the people we've got here and almost anyone that we've heard about."

Yes, I had a knack for this kind of code. I had a lot of scripts, aka bots, in my virtual toolbox to do all kinds of automated tasks, and when TOS needed this kind of thing, I was the go-to guy for it. Blackbird had seen it in action in Denver and New York—and both times I'd stopped them with my skill.

The trick would be designing a bot that looked like it would do what Blackbird wanted while at the same time not. It would be near impossible because Westside would be on the lookout for that.

I was so screwed.

"Looking at this code," I said, since if I was engaged, at least it'd look like I was trying to do what he wanted, "I see a few areas to bolster it to maintain its control. But eventually, at least in any truly secure system, there'd be measures in place to take care of any intrusion. On top of that you'd be looking at so many different scenarios that it would be almost impossible to write a single bot to take on everything."

"I'm glad you at least see something in this. It proves we should've made sure to capture you back in July."

Oh, great. I've made him happy.

"I'm going to introduce you to the team this afternoon, so you can get to work," he said as he tapped a few keys on his phone. The office door opened, and the guard stepped in. "I've told the project leaders that you're to be watched closely, so please don't try anything stupid."

The guard gestured for me to go out the door, and I did without saying anything to Westside. There was no need. A quip would just piss him off, and I had nothing constructive to add. I needed to think—a lot.

Back in the holding cell, Eddie was gone, but there was a thermos of soup, and someone had brought in a mini fridge stocked with soda, water, and some sandwiches on a plate covered with plastic wrap. At least I should be able to keep from getting sick again.

I lay back on the bed and stared up at the ceiling.

Even if I wanted to help, the project seemed insurmountable. Going from theory to practicality, though, terrified me. I couldn't play a role in that, but I also didn't know how to prevent it, unless I could try to lead them down wrong paths. But how long was that sustainable?

What was all that code?

The message made me jump as it appeared in my sight. I knew Coach and Dean watched because the transmitter icon displayed. It didn't lessen the surprise of the text appearing.

Code they're experimenting with. Did you understand?

No doubt I'd be looking at more of that this afternoon. Having Dean to bounce ideas off of would help, and Coach would be able to discuss overall strategy as well.

I've recorded everything, so I can look more in-depth.

He comes through yet again. *Perfect. Can you show me?*

His response was quick: *Yup. Give me a minute.*

Time to get to work and find the way to bring this down.

TWENTY-ONE

As PROMISED, Westside brought me to a conference room where three others sat, laptops open in front of them. A massive screen at the front of the room showed someone's desktop—featuring a starscape. Westside didn't introduce anyone.

Dean and I had spent the past two hours reviewing what Westside had shown in his office.

It helped looking at all the code again. Dean and I talked about possible exploits in what they'd shown me—although the eye typing drove me crazy. At least I felt prepared for whatever came next.

We decided Dean would continue to record, but it was becoming an urgency to get the phone charged. Despite the capacity of the battery, it couldn't last much longer.

The session with Westside and others on the team was three hours of fairly interesting project overview. A notebook and pen had been at my seat when I arrived in the room, and I made some notes of items I wanted to think about and maybe talk over with Dean.

As horrible as this plan was, I couldn't deny it was technically fascinating. It was a horrible plan that I couldn't help occasionally geeking out on.

What kind of person was I? I'm not supposed to like any part of this.

Maybe I didn't have to come up with an elaborate way to stop it, though. The team here couldn't figure out how to do this, and while I've got skills, I could just be one more smart person who couldn't crack it.

"Why do you think I can do this? I understand the idea and the attempts made, but this is significantly big."

"Everything we know indicates you're the guy for this." Westside walked to one of the tinted windows and looked out. "We've reviewed the work and research you've done at MIT. We know firsthand how you've thwarted us with how you destroyed the network in Denver." He turned back, and his eyes pierced into me in a way that they hadn't since I'd arrived. "You're going to figure this out."

I held his gaze while I sorted out what to say next. This was more than about me getting hurt or even killed, it was about a world full of people.

"How do I know you'll keep your word if it turns out I can't do what you want? Just because you think I can doesn't mean it's true."

I kept it earnest. Part of me was legit scared that I'd fail, and my friends would be targets.

"Do you need other people? Tell us who they are. If they're TOS people, we've got most of them and maybe you can persuade them to work with us. If it's somebody else, we'll go get them."

He wasn't giving an inch.

He nodded while looking to the guards at the door. Before I could react, the guards had me zip tied to the chair

—arms bound at the wrist and legs just above the ankle. My reflexes were usually better. Maybe I wasn't fully recovered.

"What the hell?" Frustration boomed through my voice. "I wasn't doing anything."

"You're looking for a way out. Your immediate concern should be getting to work." He went to his laptop clicked a few keys. "Remember, I told you about this?"

Soft music filled the room from speakers that must be hidden in the ceiling.

Not this!

Invisible daggers drove into my brain.

I closed my eyes against the searing pain and tried to not call out.

When it didn't stop, I focused on him as the fury built.

The ties were tight, but I thrashed anyway. The plastic dug into my bare wrists and hurt. The guards must've been holding the chair because I couldn't rock it.

The irritation flooding my head intensified. The song wasn't louder, but the affect increased.

Every muscle tensed as I tried to break the restraints. My chest tightened, and I gasped for air.

What the hell is happening?

The message from Dean and Coach only infuriated me more.

"Stop." It came out as a rough growl.

If I could get loose, I could take them all.

That would make it stop.

Westside silenced the music, and I slumped, chin dropping to chest.

Evil audio. I typed while I looked down so no one would see my eye movements. *Explain later.*

The effect hurt far worse than before as did my desire to do some damage. No one else in the room was impacted.

No doubt the Blackbird agents were tested to make sure they weren't susceptible to the sound.

"Imagine the tone played in the background of your school's announcements or at a McKinley game," he said. I looked up to glare at him. "Think of the damage that would be done. Your high school has fifteen hundred and thirty-one students and seventy to ninety staff depending on time of day. Our current data indicates that 22 percent of the people would react accordingly. Three or four minutes and there'd be many injuries and possibly fatalities."

He had me more than I'd thought he did. He could go after anyplace or anyone I cared about.

I hoped I had the smarts to stop this and keep everyone safe.

"And don't forget," he continued, "I can turn this on any time. And if we restrain you, it hurts worse because you can't release the tension it's causing."

His fingers were poised over the keyboard as we held each other's gaze.

"When do we start?" I finally said, sounding confident instead of defeated. I refused to give him defeated.

"Exactly the spirit we're looking for. I've got a secure workspace put together for you alongside some of the other crew. You won't be on a terminal with internet access, but we've got a test area set up. The team can run tests for you in real time if necessary, but they'll check your work first."

Another nod from Westside had the guards cutting the ties. In the short time I struggled I'd cut into my wrists, and I bled in a couple of spots.

"You know this isn't something that's gonna come together in a day, right?"

I hoped he had realistic expectations and didn't think I asked as a way to stall.

"Yes. We've been at this a while and while you're good, we don't expect miracles. As long as the reports are that you're working toward the goal, it's all good. If it at all appears you're dragging your feet or trying to double cross us, it'll get bad fast." Westside closed his laptop and the others did the same. "We'll get you started first thing tomorrow. For now you can consider what you've seen and get some more rest. The doctor tells me that's important."

I kept hold of the notebook and pen I had, and no one took it from me as I was escorted out.

Are you okay? I was asked as I went down the hall toward the elevator.

I responded since no one was looking straight at me: *Yeah. Just rattled. You get everything? Review tonight?*

Got it all. Let me know what you want to see and when. Glad to see you've got paper. That should help a lot.

I'd have to make sure to rest and not spend the whole night analyzing. No way I could afford to get sick again.

TWENTY-TWO

THE ROOM the guard escorted me to the next morning could've belonged on the MIT campus. Many workstations —some people with two or three monitors and computers around them, whiteboards lining the walls and a giant screen up front. People were hard at work when I arrived a little after eight.

The guard introduced me to a group of four—each of whom had a codename—who had worked on a control mechanism that had limited success in testing. Three women and one guy who said they were grad students at Caltech. They didn't say anything else about their back-grounds, and they didn't seem to care about my capabilities. We just dove in.

I listened closely, asked questions and provided ideas— but looked for loopholes. Anything I could exploit to thwart Westside's plan.

I learned more about the others in the room as the morning continued. Somehow Blackbird had convinced a number of people that singular control of the internet was a good thing. There were a couple dozen people in this room, and still others went in and out, seeming to consult before retreating to wherever they worked.

Some of them seemed convinced this project was important and would be a turning point for the world—some because it would get people off devices, and others wanted to control the flow of information. Two, however, were here for the same reason I was—threats.

The group ranged in age from midtwenties to midfifties. Apparently, my arrival had been heralded as what the team needed.

The assembled people reminded me of the research projects I'd been involved with at MIT. It was also a lot like being on a hockey team where we all had the same goal and each brought our particular skill set to help achieve it.

Only I didn't want to be on this team.

I kept my concentration on getting up to speed. Knowing what they were doing would hopefully unlock ideas for how to stop it. Permanently.

Internet access was limited to certain people, and the room was monitored by several mic'd cameras. Anything discussed about the project took place in this room, or a similar one, and those of us who were here against our will wouldn't have the chance to be alone together.

Given the brainpower that I'd met, I returned to the idea that what Westside wanted couldn't be done.

Could I actually figure out how to do what he wanted—either solo or with others in the group? Westside said he wasn't expecting miracles, but I suspected there was a shelf life on how long I could work without results.

A message from Dean flashed up: *We need a better way to communicate.*

He was right. How Dean and Coach made heads or tails out of what they saw was a mystery to me.

When I was at my workstation alone to review some proposed specifications, a lightning bolt of an idea struck.

You connected to my phone?

Dean responded back quick: *Yeah. It's the link to the lenses.*

It took forever to type what I needed to, but there was no choice: *I was on security cameras. Find that and tap in. This room has a mic. Do it soon. Phone can't last much longer.*

A headache started to build from all the eye movement to generate the message.

The reply came back simply: *On it.*

The amount of infrastructure Blackbird managed to set up and the amount of code deployed was staggering. They'd gotten around a lot of security measures. The team had to be larger than the people working in this building. I'd imagine there were operatives at key companies across all levels of the internet.

In the presentations, they said they believed everything was in place except the central control panel. If I could poke holes in that idea, it might provide more time.

When I couldn't sit any longer, I stood and immediately a guard came to me. This happened when any of the captives moved.

In this case, I required the guard because I needed to go to the restroom.

So far, they treated me well. It seemed that way for the others who were forced to be here. They'd put the extra furniture in my room. No one harassed me because I needed to step out. They even had snacks and drinks in the workroom.

This could've been a job—except I couldn't leave the building.

Holy crap!

As I exited, a woman I'd swear was Split Screen entered. If she recognized me, she didn't let on, and I checked my own reaction. Was she with these guys? She didn't have a guard with her, which meant she wasn't a captive like I was.

While I was at hockey camp over the summer, she'd been deployed. As per protocol, I didn't know what her mission was, but would she have ended up here? TOS had already lost at least one Blackbird embedded agent over the summer. Or was she a Blackbird double agent?

So many questions. So much didn't make sense.

The guard waited outside the single occupancy restroom.

I discontinued the video feed while I was in the bathroom, but I typed as I took care of business.

Ask D-Man if he knows the last-known location of Split Screen.

Before I could send it, the interface shut down.

Damn.

Props to the phone. It'd lasted far longer than I thought it could.

I had no idea if Dean had retrieved what he needed from the phone to get into the security system. Hopefully he'd work some more magic.

I finished up, so I wasn't in the bathroom too long. Split Screen and I had to talk. Friend or foe—knowing what to expect from her would be critical.

Back in the work room, Split Screen conferred with two people that I'd been told were in charge. Wildcat and Cobb looked like they could also be grad students, and they were whip smart in briefing me.

Split Screen fit right in with them. I'd loved working

with her during the Glenwood Music case. She'd been new to the agency then and brilliant. We'd complemented each other well.

I went back to my desk and discovered a new file had been deposited on the desktop. I didn't have outbound connectivity, but there was inbound so they could push files to me. If I had anything for them, someone came to enter a password. So far, I hadn't been able to catch the password or have time to try to hack into the broader network.

The way that desks were arranged, someone could easily see over my shoulder, so looking for a way to get online wasn't something I could chance—at least not yet.

I looked at the new folder, which was labeled *Attempted Control Systems from Quarterflash*. Inside were several files and a text file called *ReadMe*. I clicked on that as the obvious place to start.

Wildcat asked me to assemble the most promising work I'd done on an overall control system. I'd recommend looking at 3JT-X12 first.

That file name was one Split Screen and I used working previously. She'd picked it because it sounded like a ray gun name from a '50s sci-fi movie. Hopefully she had information for me.

It was a well-documented file—something Split Screen excelled at. Documentation was important when collaborating and from what I'd seen so far, not everyone in this group seemed to understand that.

The program she wrote didn't seem to have control features but was attempting to catalog everything on the web in an effort to know how large the universe was.

Interesting approach.

Almost like a search engine index, only this wasn't gathering pages but individual IP addresses.

She'd indicated a couple of subroutines where she was having trouble, so I poured over those.

There was something here.

She embedded extra material in the code.

I didn't see it at first, but going over the specific area she'd called out I soon found what she'd done.

I couldn't write this down, even though I had paper. To leave a trail would be dangerous for both of us. I had to piece together her message in my head. I went back to the top of the section and read through carefully.

Can't contact HQ. Not sure why. Rumors are Blackbird struck. Will find a way for us to talk.

I went over the message again to make sure I'd seen everything.

With her apparently on the leadership team with Wildcat and Cobb, she might have the leverage to make it so we could talk. I spent the remainder of the day adding details on how I thought she could boost the reliability of the code. I also left a response.

TOS severely compromised. Ready to talk when you are.

I went on to review and comment on the rest of the code she'd given me.

TWENTY-THREE

By the end of the day, it was difficult to think straight after all the information I'd taken in.

Of course, I knew how the internet worked, and IP addresses ruled all. From a home computer to individual websites to vast server pools, everything had an IP address that was used to route information from one place to another.

Individual internet service providers all had their own addresses to assign, companies had ones to distribute inside their own networks. But there was no top of the pyramid and over the years the systems had become more robust to prevent failure.

When you get down to the IP level and tried to catalog, as Blackbird wanted, the complexity became mind-boggling. In Westside's vision, he'd be able to control connectivity so he could turn off whatever targets—large or small—were desired. That flexibility made the system requirements crazy complicated.

This team, especially those closest to Westside, believed

it possible. Surely, they would've spoken up by now if they didn't think that—unless everyone was too scared of saying so. I hoped Split Screen could eventually shed some light on this.

An idea I considered sharing with the group involved unleashing a virus that could subvert security and give Blackbird the ability to control internet access of the infected network. The problem would be ensuring its penetration. If Blackbird had agents inside major companies like Google, Facebook, Netflix, and the like, it'd spread across the infrastructure fairly quickly. Other things would be harder, like getting it into utility networks because of the extra security in place. There were other gaps in the plan too—getting into countries that heavily restricted the net, like China, or areas where there was already little connectivity.

I didn't want to offer any ideas, but I couldn't risk the consequences. At least while working on the virus I could also design a way for it to take Blackbird out.

I got up from my desk and a guard came promptly over.

"Sorry. Standing to stretch and to use the whiteboard."

I don't know what she expected. It'd be silly for me to put up a fight since there were three guards in this room, not to mention the other consequences.

As I stretched, she went back to the door.

On the board, I drew some rough schematics of how the internet was connected, and more ideas clicked into place about the pseudo-virus. Cyberterrorists often used viruses that were triggered on a certain day unless you paid them off. That was essentially Blackbird's plan but on a larger scale.

As my scribbles took over another whiteboard, Split Screen and two others approached.

"What are you working on here? I get the small-scale networking diagram, but I can't decipher the broader purpose." I didn't know if Split Screen had been in the field previously, but she was smooth. I'd never needed to take on another persona before, and she did it flawlessly.

I went through everything, and the trio listened intently. "Is this really possible given the some 340 trillion trillion IP's just in IPv6 alone?" Split Screen fixed me with a questioning gaze.

"For IPv6, there's a trillion in there that you missed. We could just call it 340 undecillion. Regardless, only a small fraction of the addresses are in use." I couldn't resist a smile as she nodded. "If we write the scripts correctly, we should be able to send them directly to the addresses we want. The scripts would be designed to have the information required to block the traffic as well as to defend itself and take instruction from us."

Split Screen traded nods with her colleagues, and they let me keep talking without questions. "Having the IP mappings you're already working on will help because if there are specific targets to go after first, we can do that once we test all of this, since it's only hypothesis right now."

"We should build in a way to report status as well so we know the script is still in place and functional—especially if it's in a standby mode." The guy who spoke was in cargo shorts and a rumpled Pearl Jam sweatshirt. He looked excited behind his circular glasses. "I'm Cornerstone," he said.

I nodded and wrote his suggestion on the board. "Good call out. I hadn't worked my way to reporting yet, but we can add in whatever we think is necessary."

"Do we have to account for all the IPs or just the ones we're cataloging?" asked Cobb, also dressed casually in jeans and a light sweater with her blondish brown hair in a ponytail.

"The specifications are to control everything," Split Screen answered, not taking her eyes off the whiteboard. She looked exactly like she had when we worked online previously. She was always in a T-shirt that had something to do with books, and her glasses were perched on top of her head. I'd never seen her actually wear them. "I'm Quarter-flash by the way."

"And to your point," I said, looking to Cornerstone, "getting information back from them is going to be crucial. You can imagine a government facility, like the CDC, will be extra tough to get into, and stay, in their private network, so status information is a must."

"What do you think it would take to write these?" Split Screen asked, shifting her gaze to me.

"I'm not sure. I'm not even completely sure it'll work."

"It's the best idea we've had in a while," she said. "We should build and test it. I've got some ideas already we should look at incorporating."

It's either good that Split Screen stepped up to help because we can plan together. Or she's really a Blackbird agent and her direct involvement will only make it harder for me to sabotage them.

"For now our work is here," I said, gesturing to the whiteboard. "We're not to the stage we can write any code. There's a lot of requirements left to sort."

I handed her a marker, which she immediately took.

"Any of you who have ideas, throw them out," she said. "This thing isn't going to get written by just the two of us."

There were murmurs of consideration as the people around us continued to look at the board. She gave a slight nod to me. I didn't return it, but I hoped it meant we were on the same page.

TWENTY-FOUR

Smart people working together to achieve a goal was my favorite thing to be part of.

Except when it was to take over the world.

Terrifying didn't even begin to cover how I felt about this.

I finally returned to my room... cell... prison.... I wasn't sure what to call it. I'd spent about twelve hours in the workroom and the scribbles on the whiteboard seemed to dance in front of my eyes.

I kept the late dinner simple with a grilled chicken salad. It made sense to eat right to keep up my strength, especially since I'd been so sick. I've never been one who binged on the wrong food during fits of work. Sure there was a lot of Dr Pepper and maybe some late-night snacks of Nutter Butter cookies or Doritos. But I tried to keep the major meals in check.

I came up with some additional ideas and writing them down in the notebook was restrictive. I didn't mind making notes on paper, but without whiteboards and computers things got unruly fast.

I decided to go back to the workroom for just a little bit. Rest was important, and I didn't want to ignore sleep—at least not yet. The guard didn't seem to mind the return trip upstairs.

I returned to the whiteboard and surveyed what we'd written earlier. I added a few more concepts on how to breach private networks while looking for places I could sabotage everything. I went to my desk and pulled up the information about the IP directories that had been created. In particular I was curious about how far they'd gone with government and utilities.

At the bottom of the screen, text appeared letter by letter—an incoming message.

Locksmith here. Can see and hear you. Can finally message too and I'll see everything you type.

Whoa!

Dean again goes above and beyond.

Hopefully I didn't betray anything to the cameras, although it was tempting to look up and smile.

How?

Security system gave me enough access to poke around. I was able to figure out which computer was yours, and I removed the restriction keeping you off the network. They shouldn't be able to detect it as long as you don't do anything crazy.

You are my hero.

I immediately felt better with the outside connection reestablished. It remained a priority to get my phone, though. Getting the lenses back up would let them see more accurately than the broad view of the cameras.

How much do you know?

I anxiously waited for the response. As frustrating as the three dots on an iPhone can be during a text message, there is nothing quite like watching the message form letter by letter, with frequent backspaces, because Dean wasn't the best typist.

Most of the day. We've been recording what's said in the room, so we can keep track of it. For what it's worth, the plan makes sense to me even though it's scary as hell. How can I help stop it?

Part of me hoped the plan didn't make sense. At least it would buy time as I worked on the more critical plan to destroy Blackbird.

Dean could do a lot from his vantage point. We needed to know if we could take down Blackbird's infrastructure just like they'd done with TOS.

I typed what I needed him to do, especially looking for data transfers between here and servers that might also be Blackbird's. I couldn't believe Westside was the mastermind. Less than a year ago, he seemed to be a hotheaded analyst, and here he'd morphed into one of their leaders.

The bolt on the door clicked, and Westside walked in. According to the clock at the top of the monitor it was after midnight. I would've suspected that he'd be home in bed rather than showing up to see me.

"I like this. Shows you're committed. I had good reports today about your contributions. How about walking me through it?"

I stole a look at the monitor, and whatever control Dean had on this computer, he was able to cover it up quick because none of our conversation showed. It was only the code that I'd been looking through.

"Sure. It'd be good to get another perspective."

Why not play along?

I started with what had spurred my idea and went on for about an hour. He even asked smart questions, but there was no additional input into any of it. Maybe this was outside his area of expertise.

"I can see why people were impressed," Westside said. "How long will this take?"

The magic question.

"No timelines yet. We're still stepping through the structure for the scripts. We're likely to only get one chance to deploy, so it has to be correct. If there are too many signs of a disruption, we'll be shut down before we get started. To that end, we've also got to find a way to test it before any full-scale deployment."

He nodded and looked to the boards thoughtfully.

"You know, I have to wonder." He turned and drew a small gun from his waistband. I hadn't seen it earlier because his shirt was untucked. He aimed at my head. I took two steps back before running into a desk. "Have you duped everyone like you did in Denver? Is there something in here that none of us can find? I've let everybody know that anything you provide has to be thoroughly vetted."

The guard at the door didn't even flinch. Her stoic facade left no doubt she wouldn't intervene on whatever Westside planned.

Maybe I should've been scared, but I'd had my Dad point a gun at me a year ago and been shot even earlier this year. While my pulse sped up, the threat didn't really faze me. I'd been through too much to allow it.

Westside and I locked eyes, and he kept the gun steady. We'd had staring contests in Denver, except this time there was no one to force us to stop. No way he'd shoot me; he still needed my work.

"I'm curious. Why haven't you just forced me to do this with the mind control tech? I'm assuming you've recovered that and continue to develop it."

A smile broke across his face—a creepy one that lay somewhere between a Cheshire cat and someone trying too hard to look innocent. "Believe me I wish that were possible. We have all the technology, and we've been developing it. Unfortunately it renders the controlee able to only execute instructions. We haven't figured out a way to get someone's intelligence, creativity, and thought processes to work under our control. Perhaps you can assist with that once we're done with this."

He'd offered far more information than I expected. At least I didn't have to worry about the mind control like I did the horrible audio tech. The prospect of staying here after the internet project chilled me to my core.

Even if I couldn't bring this down, working for this agency was not something I'd do. Maybe I'd messed up by not setting the conditions of my release before I got started.

"Interesting. I wonder if that's why TOS shelved the project," I said. "Blindly following instructions is rarely a good thing since there's usually some judgment required."

He lowered the gun and returned it to his waistband. What I said that prompted him to do that, I don't know. At least that threat had passed.

"Yeah," he said, shifting his attitude to friendly, "it's a shame it doesn't work that easy. And we really don't know the key to getting around it. It's become a secondary project, though. Consider these scripts." He turned his attention back to the board and pointed to some of our notes about the bots' requirements. "They need to learn. So even these have some intelligence. We need the same thing in any mind control that we attempt. If all we need to do is execute simple instructions, we might as well build a robot."

He'd shared a lot. I'm glad Dean and Coach captured it.

It wouldn't help a ton, but it was good to have that documented for future review.

Westside ran his hand through his short black hair and studied the board again.

"What are your immediate next steps?"

I stepped up next to him, also looking at the drawings and notes. "Like I said, we need to finalize the requirements and start coding the framework. We've also got to figure out how to test. We don't want to break the internet in a way that we don't intend."

"Kinda like feeding a cute gremlin after dark and ending up with a bunch of evil gremlins?" Westside smiled and chuckled.

I kept my focus on the board. If Lorenzo, or another friend, had made that analogy I'd have joined in and probably offered others. No way I'd do that with him.

"I'll let you get back to work," Westside finally said. "I'll expect daily updates at six o'clock from you, Quarterflash, and Wildcat."

I nodded.

Without another word he pivoted and headed to the door. The guard unlocked it before he got there.

I continued to look at the board for several minutes, then went back to check with Dean before I called it a night.

TWENTY-FIVE

After I took a quick shower, I dropped onto the bed in a T-shirt and boxers.

I toyed with the idea that if these scripts proved successful in concept, they could be used to knock out Blackbird's network and potentially even destroy it. Even with Split Screen on the inside, she might not be able to get the right access to do the mapping. Dean, on the other hand, from the outside might be able to trace how far their connectivity extended. It would be nearly impossible to know if he got it all, but it was worth the chance to see how far he could map.

In the morning, a priority would be to figure out how to communicate with Split Screen.

I missed Eddie. It'd been nice lying next to him. I hadn't seen him since I went to the workroom yesterday morning. I didn't know if he was still locked up or if his dad took him away.

Having pushed down thoughts about him all day, it was impossible to do as I tried to drift off to sleep. I continued debating with myself if I should rescue Eddie as part of this mission. Or would it be better if he walked away on his own. Given what he'd done to me in New York, TOS might not take me bringing him out well, even though he's helped me here.

The door lock clanked as it released, and I pulled the blanket up, even though I had clothes on.

It was late, and it didn't make sense for anyone to show up.

Eddie stuck his head around the door. "You want some company?"

Wow.

"Sure." He came in, and I saw the guard pull the door closed behind him. "It's good to see you."

He hung out near the door, looking miserable, with his hands jammed in his jeans pockets. Eddie usually exuded confidence. He looked zapped.

"We're moving," he said sadly. "Dad's reassigned. He's pissed. Feels like me getting Mitch out and trying to break you out cost him a promotion. So... I guess this might be it for us."

Even though he'd left months ago under terrible circumstances, this was still a kick in the stomach. It's crazy that I'd thought there could be an us if I resolved this.

This boy held tight to my heart—and I didn't want him to let go.

He looked up and our eyes met. His were glassy as if they were on the edge of spilling over and that made my chest tighten.

"You don't have to stand way over there." And again, ignoring common sense, I opened the covers and slid back so he had space. "If this is it, let's at least get one last night."

Excitement coursed through me knowing I was about to hold him. We weren't gonna be able to do anything hard-core, but I really didn't care if the camera caught us making out. I couldn't see our situation getting any worse.

He didn't hesitate coming over, kicking his shoes off at the edge of the bed.

He nestled against me, and I wrapped my arm over his chest. Despite the time we'd spent together here, I still wasn't used to the new way he felt. I took advantage of our spooning to feel up some of his new muscles. His nearly bald head continued to surprise me. I'd never seen any pictures of him, even baby pictures, with hair so short—it was barely there. It must've been part of a disguise since he did look quite different without the Afro.

We lay silently for a while. I was hyperaware of the rise and fall of his chest. He was tense—body quite stiff—and he probably stared at the wall across from us. I waited for him to relax a little, but it didn't happen.

"Are you going to be able to fix this?" His voice was soft.

I raised one of my legs and draped it over his, trying to draw us even closer together.

"I don't know. I'm worried about what happens in either scenario."

Even if I did my best, I feared for the people I cared about.

"How do you deal with this? It's like my life's not mine anymore, but you've been doing it for years."

"Only for the last year has it been anything like this." Uncharted territory lay ahead. Eddie and I could never discuss this before, but now he was in it as much as I was. "The first five years or so I was just a tech working on network security and gadgets. Sometimes I'd help out an agent in the field, but that was at my desk. It wasn't until Denver that I was out there."

"I'm sorry for my part in all this." He pulled my arm

tighter around him and interlocked our fingers. I shifted so he could back closer into me. "I should've said no and then none of this would've happened."

I kissed the back of his head several times. "They would've done it somehow. They figured me out when they snatched me off my bike. They didn't know who they were getting, they just knew it was someone with a tracker. You saved me from that. Who knows what would've happened if you hadn't."

It felt good talking about this, but it was also painful. Butterflies in my stomach created nervous energy. I held Eddie tighter, which he seemed to like.

"What do you think happens next?" I asked. "For you, I mean."

He shrugged, which he barely had room to do. "I've no idea. I hoped Dad would send me to Mom. She'd take me, but he won't let me go because I know too much."

He shifted and because this wasn't our first time in a bed, I recognized the signs that he wanted to turn over. I moved to let that happen. I fought the urge to kiss him as we aligned face to face. This was just talk... but he was so close and with such hurt in his eyes that it was hard to not immediately try to comfort him.

"I honestly think he'd be happy if I disappeared." He shifted his gaze away from mine. He couldn't decide where to look, but he was avoiding me. Tears welled up again. "I wouldn't be surprised if he had me taken out."

Another gut punch. Could he be serious? His father would make the choice to kill him?

I'd already had my dad level a gun at me. He was under mind control at the time, but there was still that feeling of betrayal. Nothing I'd seen from Mr. Cochrane in the past made me think he could do that to Eddie. He wasn't as nice as my parents, but he seemed like he genuinely cared for Eddie and at least played the proud father around his swimming accomplishments. He even seemed to like me—and that was well before he had any idea I was an agent.

"Really?"

"I don't know." He shrugged again. "Maybe I'm wrong. I've never seen him this angry, though. Not even when I didn't capture you."

I pulled him still closer, even though it hadn't seemed possible given our positioning. He looked devastated. I'd never known a time when I didn't have the support of my parents. Eddie had lost everything—being able to see his mom, the friends he had in Boston, me. His life split apart, at least in part, because my identity had been revealed to the wrong people. I kissed his forehead because it was closest, and he shuddered a little.

"I'm so sorry."

"How can you be sorry?" His voice cracked. "I did all this to you. It's by far the worst thing I've ever done. Probably ever will do." He tried to pull away, but I wouldn't let him. "I shouldn't be here."

I wouldn't let go. "I never stopped loving you. I couldn't."

His eyes found mine, hopeful for the first time since he'd come in the room.

"What're we going to do?"

I had no answers, yet my heart soared when he said *we.*

"I don't know."

He sighed and rested his forehead against mine, and eventually we drifted off to sleep.

TWENTY-SIX

THE DOOR FLUNG open after a couple of knocks. Eddie and I jerked upright, and he threw his legs over the side of the bed as he sat up.

I hadn't heard the bolt unlock because I'd been dead asleep. It was the soundest sleep I'd had in days. Eddie and I relaxed each other like we always did. The small clock on the desk across the room read six thirty-three.

"Winger, you're needed in the work room immediately."

The guard wasn't one I recognized. He looked stern, almost annoyed that he had to provide this information. "Relay, I've been asked to keep you here until your father comes for you."

What was going on?

Eddie stood, which allowed me to get out of bed. I ignored the hard-on in my boxers, giving it one adjustment to make sure it stayed out of sight.

I pulled on jeans and one of the black long-sleeved shirts I'd been provided. Eddie, who'd sat back on the bed, watched silently. At least he looked calmer. He was either ready to accept whatever came next, or he had a plan.

I wanted to know which, but I couldn't ask.

The guard looked more impatient as I got into socks and sneakers, but I wasn't going to let him push me to go faster. I crossed back to Eddie, pulled him up, and leaned into him with my head planted in its usual spot on his right shoulder. He wrapped his arms around me. I looked up, and he leaned down and planted a kiss on my lips. We hadn't done more than snuggle last night so the energy of this kiss vibrated through me all the way to my toes.

The guard cleared his throat as it continued. "They're waiting, Winger. The longer they wait, the less happy they'll be."

We let the kiss run its course. Our connection seemed as strong as ever as we pulled back at the same time.

"Take care of yourself," I said, looking into his eyes.

"You too," he said before giving me another quick kiss. "This is just a 'see ya later.'"

I nodded. If I said anything, I'd explode into a million pieces, and this wasn't the time.

Knowing that Eddie was trying to stay positive even after what he'd said last night overwhelmed me but gave me faith too. He said it with the confidence that I loved. I needed that since I still wasn't seeing a good resolution.

"You should go," he finally said with a slight smirk, as I still held on.

I nodded and backed my way to the door, not taking my eyes off him until I entered the hallway and the guard closed the door.

The guard was silent as he trailed behind me.

Inside, the room buzzed with activity. I was glad to be summoned so I could keep up with what was going on.

The whiteboards I'd worked on yesterday had new annotations and had spilled over to new boards that had been wheeled into place alongside the ones mounted to the wall. Half a dozen people were on computers furiously typing away. Westside was here too, talking with Cobb, Wildcat, and Split Screen—I couldn't bear to call her Quarterflash.

The energy was intense but also purposeful. Something had changed the vibe in the room from yesterday.

"Winger, join us." Westside was ridiculously happy, and I cringed. He'd figured something out. I braced for the worst.

"After we chatted a few hours ago, I couldn't get back to sleep because you'd sparked so many ideas," he said as he broke away from the group. He went to the whiteboard and grabbed a marker. "Here, let me show you."

I joined him as Split Screen and the others filled in around us.

"I've already been through this a little with these guys, but now that you're here, I'll step through all of it."

He talked—a lot. Some of it was what we'd talked about earlier but there were new concepts. I stayed silent, but some others, including Split Screen, weighed in with additional ideas or called out where the logic was wonky. At least they weren't all yes-men. As the suggestions and input came, he adjusted what was on the board.

After how volatile he was in Denver, it surprised me he could work in a team like this.

The concepts looked solid, and he'd proposed a structure for the code—so it could learn from mistakes—and not just for the individual bots but the entire network we'd deploy so it would get stronger as it spread out.

"Winger?"

Split Screen snapped me out of my thoughts. I looked between her, the board, and Westside, who was looking expectantly at me.

"I asked for your opinion," Westside said with a tinge of annoyance.

"Sorry, I was considering what would be needed to create this while keeping it small enough to travel easily." I scribbled on the boards in a different color to keep my notes separate. "We always knew the AI would have to learn fast and this logic makes sense. I'd make some adjustments here." As always, I looked for ways to bring this all down. With so many working on the project, I'd have to be careful to keep my work hidden.

"How soon?" Westside asked, focusing his attention on Split Screen, Wildcat, and Cobb. No one spoke. "Come on. The specs are all here, maybe even more than we need."

Continued silence led his smile to become more of a frown.

"I'd say it's at least a couple of days to get even something preliminary ready to test," Split Screen finally said after she studied it further. "This logic makes it even more important to have a well-controlled test to make sure we can actually turn connections on and off rather than breaking them."

"We need good targets to test," Cobb continued, "yet ones that won't raise too much suspicion. It'll need to be more than one too, since we want to make sure these scripts learn from each other."

Flashes of *Star Wars* came to mind—the scenes where they decided to test the Death Star on Alderaan. Depending on the test, so many could be affected. It wouldn't be a planet blowing up, but the results could still be disastrous.

A smirky smile returned to Westside's face.

"How much computing power is there to support this?" The question had just popped into my head, so I asked it.

"Terra?" Westside looked behind me, and I followed his gaze to a woman at the back of the assembled group.

"All this AI is going to need a supporting infrastructure. I'll need specs to make sure there's more than we need. With the cloud services we have access to, capacity, in theory, shouldn't be a problem as long as we're networked right. We also have to make sure we don't block our own servers."

That might be an area to exploit. It'd depend entirely on how Terra ensured that wouldn't happen.

"Make sure we're ready for it," Westside said, and Terra acknowledged the request. "I want a test ready within forty-eight hours using at least a midsize bank, a hospital, and a media company. Wildcat, I want a target list in twelve hours, so we know what we're hitting."

"On it," he said.

"I'll update Odeon, and then I'll be back to check in."

As the people dispersed, I stayed behind taking in all the information. Westside had good ideas—good enough that they scared me. What Blackbird wanted would happen if we wrote the code correctly.

I had two days or less to permanently end this.

And who was Odeon? That was a new name. Was Odeon their director? In the same capacity as Raptor for TOS?

Split Screen came up beside me. "Do you see anything wrong? You're studying this very closely."

"Not wrong. It's just a lot to make a lightweight bot do. The amount of computing power will be crucial to off-load some of the computations. Terra has a lot to prepare for."

"Are you able to build the framework?" Split Screen and I turned to face each other. Her tone was snide and demeaning. I'd never seen this side of her. "I've got others who want to prove themselves, but Westside is obsessed with you doing it."

"I guess you'll find out." All the confidence I could muster went into the words.

"You've got twelve hours to present a working concept."

"Isn't that rather arbitrary?"

"Not at all. If you fail, we need time to recover from that."

"I need my phone," I blurted out. "I've got stuff on it that will help this go faster and let me do some testing as I go."

She eyed me suspiciously.

"I'll see what I can do. I'm all for speeding up the work. We'll need to check the device to make sure you can't do anything harmful." I nodded. "I suggest you get started."

She spun around and went to talk to Wildcat and Cobb while I went to my workstation. Opening one of the notebooks I'd used yesterday, I wrote out the basic structure of what I needed to build.

TWENTY-SEVEN

THE LONGER I sat in front of the computer and Dean remained silent, the more worry tugged on me. I'd been handwriting notes on the requirements for some twenty minutes, and he'd said nothing.

I typed a single character: ?

Returning to the notebook, I burned another ten or so minutes and still nothing from the outside world.

Something was wrong.

Dean and Coach had been on for hours, and it didn't make sense for them to suddenly go dark, unless they were booted out of the system or captured.

No one here acted like the system has been compromised.

Disturbing.

Suddenly a green dot appeared in the upper right corner of my vision. The contacts returned to transmission mode. Split Screen had stepped out while I'd been spec'ing out my code. She must've talked to Westside about the phone and someone had plugged it in.

She knew TOS phones as well as I did, so she'd be able to keep them out of the sensitive areas while validating there were code snippets and test programs to help the project. Plus, as far as Blackbird knew, my computer wasn't online, but if the hole Dean had punched was still there, the phone should be able to find it and act as a beacon for Dean or anyone else from TOS.

There wasn't much I could do but proceed, so I started coding. As I typed an additional letter flashed next to each character. It barely stayed on screen long enough for me to see. If I was a typist who looked at the keys, or somewhere else, I'd have missed it.

Without being able to write it down, I had to keep track of what I saw. I typed slow, so I wouldn't miss the letter that flashed on the screen. As usual, Dean was smart. He'd started with *Winger Message* and repeated it three times to ensure I'd catch on before he got to the important part.

<Message>D-man says we're compromised and must move. Got most of network mapped. It's on your computer as hidden part of IP directory. Password is bully. Back online asap.</message>

Jesus.

If they found Dean and Coach, would they go for Mitch again or Iris or....

I shoved that out of my head. My focus had to be on ending this project.

The network diagram Dean made would wait. There were too many people in here to risk looking at it now. I got back to my task and split time between writing the real code and adding hidden destructive routines.

After an hour or so, I ended up at the whiteboards again writing some high-level information the other teams needed to know so they could integrate into my framework. I also got exact details on what each group worked on.

Split Screen finally turned up with my phone and beckoned me back to my workstation. Nothing had changed with the feed transmitting from the lenses, so if she knew they were working she didn't tamper with that app. That meant the phone was still online too.

"Westside, myself, and two other techs have examined the phone, and we've disabled its ability to get online." She sounded utterly convincing. I'd have to ask her sometime how she unlocked it because it shouldn't have been that easy. "You can use whatever files are here on your terminal only. The rest of the team knows not to allow this to be connected to their machines."

"Understood."

Having the phone so close gave me the jitters because it opened up more options to end this. I just had to be smart on how I used it.

"Based on our analysis, it looks like you want to use what's in this folder." She put the phone on the desk, already opened to a set of apps—exactly the apps I'd been refining for years to help me write new bots quickly. Many were in the TOS library, but some, ones I hadn't released yet because they weren't ready for general use, were also there.

Something new sat alongside everything else.

Beta 5

We discussed several of the apps, including two of the betas, but she skipped five. She'd matched my naming convention, so it looked like it belonged. It turned out to be a good thing that I'd only numbered these, which I'd done because I didn't want to be bothered with coming up with more descriptive names.

Before she left, I updated her on what I'd done in the past couple of hours and what my next tasks were. It'd give her something to report back.

Her facade didn't crack even a millimeter. She was good at this undercover thing. I wondered if I ever would be, or if I'd even get the chance.

"Looks good, Winger. I'll have Westside review this, so he can see the good work you're doing."

I gave a simple nod.

Going back and forth between my coding and occasionally consulting on other components of the project, I kept a running list of ideas on sabotage.

Six hours passed at turbo speed, and I hadn't had the chance to do two key things—check out what I'd gotten from Dean and Split Screen.

How to test my schemes troubled me. I had no way to prove anything would work. With Dean unresponsive, I couldn't even talk it through with him.

I'd written in a backdoor that would destroy the system. Everyone would know I did it, but I couldn't let that stop me from executing it if I needed to. I built the trigger into the contact lenses so that I'd be able to engage it in almost any circumstance.

Even with the deadline, it finally got to the point where most people left for the day. I could finally check Dean's data.

Dean took great precautions to shield the work he provided from anybody else. He'd structured the reports to look like the IP directory that Blackbird had already assembled.

The Blackbird network was quite similar to TOS with a few central hubs and a lot of dispersed networking relying heavily on cloud resources. They also followed the TOS standard of not having a clear top of the hierarchy. Since they were trying to safeguard the network, Split Screen might be able to provide information that I could compare to Dean's info. Nothing would make me happier than knocking out the entire operation.

The best plan would seek out everything on the network and wipe it out. Destruction poised a problem, though—that would likely wipe out the Blackbird agent list. Saving the internet and taking out the primary threat was important, but they'd gone after TOS people and they had to answer for that too.

I put away everything I'd looked at related to the network and cleaned up my tracks.

Moving over to Split Screen's file, I discovered it wasn't an app at all but a carefully disguised file with a message.

Winger, good call getting your phone back. I hadn't realized you had it here or I would've gotten it back a while ago because this gives us a secure way to communicate. I'm here undercover. They think they recruited me out of Norton because of the networking projects I'd done. I know you must be working on a way to shut this down. TOS orders have been that if we can't shut it down reasonably that we must cause mass destruction of their infrastructure. Raptor says either is acceptable. I've got the agent list but can't send to TOS because of the network issue.

The details for keeping the Blackbird network safe, I think, is the key to stopping this, and I think you do too. I'm looking at the network diagrams this evening, and I'll upload them here too. We'll have to write to each other here. Everything is mic'd, so we can't talk.

I know we can do this. We took care of business with

Glenwood. Write me back when you can. I've got a notification built-in, so I'll know when you do.

Before I called it a night, I wrote back that the diagrams were exactly what I needed.

There was finally a tiny beacon of light at the end of this dark tunnel.

TWENTY-EIGHT

I sat up with a scream—actually I wasn't sure if it was out loud or only in my head.

My legs were tangled, and the sheet had come untucked from the foot of the bed.

Catching my breath proved difficult and painful. It felt like I'd done suicide sprints on the ice for hours.

Once I focused I realized my location—the cell Blackbird kept me in.

After I'd turned in my initial framework to Split Screen just under the twelve-hour mark, she recommended I rest while they reviewed. I'd eaten some pizza and took the opportunity to grab some sleep.

I'd been more tired than I thought. Drifting off had been easy.

But the dream—confused, crazy snatches of things.

John bleeding on the floor....

Eddie looking down at me after he'd drugged me....

Mitch held captive....

Finding Coach on the roof before that rescue....

Dad with his gun on me....

There were things I didn't recognize too.

Scenes of me working alongside people I didn't know....

The chaos of a world without the internet....

Banks messed up....

Blackouts because energy networks fail....

People dying because medical records can't be accessed....

Past, present, and possible future mixed with screams of my names—both Winger and Theo.

They asked me to do more... to make it stop... to fix it.

I almost fell out of bed trying to get untangled. Once I did, I drew my legs up to my chest and leaned against the wall.

This was what a panic attack felt like. I'd had emotional outbursts before, but this was amped up.

Blackbird even running tests was wrong. Even a small number of targets could be catastrophic for the people impacted.

If I couldn't stop it, what did that mean for the world?

I wasn't in this alone. Split Screen worked on it to, but could I fully trust her? I'd know soon.

Was anyone working on this from the outside. It'd been five days since Lorenzo pinged me. And even though it had only been a day since I had contact with Dean and Coach, it felt like the world had closed in.

Eddie was gone too.

I'd asked the guard when I returned if he knew anything. He just shook his head.

Precious few people knew where I was—Coach, Eddie, and Mitch. If Split Screen hadn't been able to report in before the TOS network went out, no one would know her whereabouts either.

Even awake and with the dream in the past, my lungs were tight, and my heart thumped loud and fast.

I couldn't stop rocking.

Was it better to stand up and walk around or sit and try to take deep breaths?

At least I wasn't doing this in front of anybody—other than whoever watched the camera.

There were options—always. Any program could be rewritten to accomplish the goal. This was not a no-win scenario.

The key was figuring it out fast enough.

My track record for doing that was solid so far—if only I could be sure this time. If I screwed it up, the consequences were unimaginable. If the internet takedown doesn't happen and they blamed that on me or my code....

How I brought this to an end had to be total. It also had to result in the capture of those responsible, so my friends were safe.

Eddie was on my mind too. Even though he double-crossed me, he ended up in that position because he knew me. I can't imagine what it was like for him to find out from his father what I did and then be forced to act like nothing had changed between us. He'd kept his cover perfectly—clearly better than I did. There was nothing I pinpointed, right up to the moment he walked out on me in New York, that gave away the secret he'd carried.

Complete and absolute destruction was required.

Just like Dean had destroyed the laptop at the computer science competition....

That's what I had to do.

I stood and quickly got dressed.

It had to be bigger than what Dean did since I'd target a number of computers, and I didn't know exactly where they were located. But I think Dean provided what I needed to execute the final move.

I knocked on the door, so I could be escorted back to the workroom.

It was possible I'd make a huge mess doing this, but I'd take the chance. Since Split Screen had the agent list, it would be possible to round people up—if not for TOS than other authorities.

And if there was collateral damage along the way, that could be cleaned up far easier than a global internet outage.

The guard opened the door and simply nodded before he stood aside so I could walk in front toward the elevators. If I did this right, it'd be the last time I made this trip.

TWENTY-NINE

Split Screen, Cobb, and Wildcat weren't present when I arrived in the workroom, but plenty of others huddled around keyboards. After a few minutes consulting with someone charged with integrating AI components, I took the time to check on some things.

Dean hadn't returned, but I could proceed without him. My phone sat on the desk, where I'd left it, connected with the standard lightning cable connection to the computer. If I could access the way Dean had gotten into the computer, I'd be able to pair it with the phone to accomplish my plan. I opened some command line windows and typed.

I poked around the open connections to the phone and found the outbound connection Dean had opened.

The networking information from Split Screen and Dean would help me lock on to all the right computers with a destructive script. I wished I could place a TOS phone next to every computer. The same EMP that I neutralized my tracker chip with could be used to wipe disc drives and completely fry the hardware.

Since I couldn't create an EMP in all the networked

computers, I'd refine what Dean had done—go after the power supplies and force a surge. If the surge couldn't happen for any reason, the bot would force the unit to over-heat and reformat the hard disk.

At the same time, the bot would send back a GPS location that I'd store—somewhere I'd have to figure out—so agents could be dispatched to recover anything still there. It'd be better if people were ready to make arrests, but there was no time to orchestrate that.

Westside, Split Screen, Wildcat, and Cobb returned. Split Screen didn't look my way. I could clue her into my plan, but if she had flipped to Blackbird's side, my access would get shut down. I wouldn't take that risk since I didn't know when I'd have this chance again.

Even if I told her, she likely couldn't help because it might get suspicious if she and I worked together. It was already difficult to code in the middle of the room and not get found out.

Still, if I brought her into the loop, I might get access to her TOS phone. The combined power of our phones would easily take out the electronics inside this building unless they were shielded. The attack would then be two pronged —my bots for the external computers and an EMP wiping out this facility. I needed to run a sweep for Split Screen's phone, so I could tie it into mine and the contact lenses for control.

There might be some electronics outside the building that got fried, potentially the streetlights or equipment in the building next door, but most of the damage would stay contained.

"Winger." Westside startled me. I looked up from my monitor as he approached. "Your framework looks mostly solid. There are a couple things I'm going to go over with these guys, but there's no reason we can start integrating."

"Yeah," Cobb added, coming in behind him, "we were sure you were gonna try to sneak something in there, but not only does it look like it will do what we need, it's actually more fortified then we expected."

What I'd built in stayed under the radar. The task hadn't been easy, and I'd pushed myself with my coding technique. My professors would be impressed.

"What's the integration plan?" I asked.

"You and Cornerstone will lead the efforts," Split Screen said. "It's your framework, and he has the most knowledge of everything we're trying to do, so that should make the work go fast. We expect to run the first test by this time tomorrow."

Crap. I wanted this to end today and I hadn't expected a buddy. More challenges to keeping my work hidden.

"Terra's working so we'll have the infrastructure in place tonight," Split Screen continued. "Assembling servers with various functionalities so we can try turning off their IP's. We'll also hit the targets outside our network to validate. Let's get to work so our timeline doesn't change."

Cornerstone followed me to my desk. "Are you going to be sticking around after Override's complete?" he asked as he brought his chair over.

"I have no idea what they plan to do with me once we're finished," I said. The nervous quiver was more for cover because, regardless of outcome, I wasn't going to stay.

"You're cool to work with, so I hope you stay." Cornerstone seemed to be in his middle twenties, and I had to admit he was good to collaborate with. "I'll put in a good word for you if I can. Seems a shame that they would get rid of someone as obviously talented as you are. And it's gonna be pretty epic if we pull this off. It'll make a lot of money for all of us."

How could Cornerstone not see the big picture?

Did he think much of the money would flow into his pocket? That was for whoever ran all this with *maybe* some bonus pay to those close to the top. I wouldn't be surprised if most of the project team was wiped out too, so they wouldn't go bragging about what they'd done or try to undo it once they figured out how bad the impact was.

It surprised me Cornerstone could be so blind to consequences of what we were doing.

Ultimately tomorrow's test had to provide a perfect cover to destroy everything.

THIRTY

NOT BEING able to test any aspect of my code made me increasingly anxious to the point that I felt a little sick to my stomach. Ideally, I'd be able to give it a controlled test to ensure that it would execute the destruction I planned for Blackbird. As it is, there could be a typo that I've missed that prevents it executing.

Even in previous missions where I couldn't test, there was normally an opportunity to make refinements. This was either going to work or not, and if it failed, the odds of a second chance were slim.

This code proved to be the most complex I'd assembled on the fly. I knew what needed to be done and the theory behind it. All the ways that I usually worked went out the window. I decided to leave Split Screen out of it so if I failed, her cover would be intact to try again.

Under the guise of confirming that we were integrating everyone's code snippets into the general framework correctly, I huddled at my keyboard. The only people who talked to me were Split Screen to check on my overall progress and Cornerstone with status updates from the teams finishing their components. Lucky for me, the artificial intelligence team was running behind.

The phone screen lit up indicating an app update. Split Screen sent a new message.

"What's that?" Cornerstone asked as he passed the desk.

Shit.

"Just saving scripts back to my library. I've created new stuff, and I want to save the snippets. You never know when they'll come in handy."

"Oh, man, great idea." He seemed excited and even more importantly didn't question my story. "I didn't even think of that."

When he dropped into his desk, I pulled up a window on my computer to read Split Screen's message.

I got the agent list out to my private cloud since I wasn't sure how safe anything else was. I wish we could talk for even five minutes away from this room, but that would be way too suspicious. I saw some extra code you'd written into the framework. No one else seemed to, but it looks like you're working on a plan. I'm working on countermeasures too, but I don't get much time at a keyboard. I hope yours works. If you think I can help, let me know.

Getting the agent list out was excellent. Hopefully we'd soon get that into the hands of people who could round them up and get TOS agents released. On the other hand, that she'd seen some of what I'd done in the framework was a concern because if she could....

I couldn't go down that rabbit hole. We'd worked together before, so of all people, she'd be the one to spot anything.

Everyone's concern at the moment focused on the AI team, because we weren't going to make our test deadline if they didn't complete soon. Cornerstone and I predicted it would take at least an hour to integrate into the framework and possibly longer.

I took one last look at everything, including the destructive code I'd unleash. I'd even tried to hide it better because of Split Screen's comment. It all looked right to me, and the trigger I'd set in the contact lenses was ready. I'd activate it as soon as the test began, and after that it could only be stopped because it completed the job or if I turned it off.

Ideally it would appear to Blackbird as though something had gone catastrophically wrong.

I also tied my phone to Split Screen's. Her TOS phone pinged from inside the building in a room on the first floor. It hadn't moved since I'd found it. The lenses would also trigger the EMP.

The last thing I set up was reporting to my cloud server. I'd have a report of what connected electronics were taken out, as well as which ones the bots couldn't affect and where they were located. I had to believe the protocols TOS had with agencies like Homeland Security, the CIA, and FBI were still in place and they could use the information even if TOS couldn't.

Cornerstone came in and dragged his chair next to my desk. "AI team is finished, and we can pick up their code." He reached around me and logged in, so he could pick up the files. He either trusted me completely or didn't care what my other windows were—he just plowed on. Thankfully, I'd already closed what he shouldn't see. "I figured we could do the final work together and get this done faster."

Split Screen and some others came over.

"How long?" Wildcat asked.

"I'd say we're still in the hour-ish time frame," I said and looked to Cornerstone who nodded eagerly.

"Good. We'll notify Westside." Wildcat left as Split Screen and Cobb went to the whiteboard and marked off some of the to-do list.

THE HOUR ZIPPED BY, and we finished getting the AI put into the overall framework and plugged into all the components that needed access to it. We also completed the review of the entire sequence.

It looked solid. Too solid.

I had confidence this would likely do everything it was designed to. My backdoors were still in place as far as I could see without digging in too much to verify.

"Looks good to me," Cornerstone said.

"Yeah. It does. Let's send it on."

I got up and let Cornerstone log in and drop the file onto the server.

Westside, Split Screen, and others immediately huddled around a monitor. Cornerstone and I came up behind them once the file was in place. From behind everyone it was impossible for me to see what specifically they were looking at.

Only a small bit of the right corner of the screen was visible, and it was too far away to read any of the text. No doubt they were reviewing the code one last time before they authorized the test.

Cornerstone leaned over and whispered, "I'm going to go make sure everything's ready with Terra. I think we did good, Winger."

"Yeah. I think we did. You need any help?" I probably shouldn't offer help, but it was better than just sitting around.

"Nah, I'm good. Besides, if there's any questions one of us should be here."

All I could do was wait.

"How's it look?" I asked, stepping through the group to get to Westside and the others.

"Some of this is really elegant for how quick it came together," Cobb said.

I winced at the unwanted compliment. On the other hand, they liked what they saw and that should keep people safe.

"I wish you could be happy about this, Winger," Split Screen said.

"I didn't really have a choice but to give it my best, did I?"

Westside locked eyes with me for a moment before looking back at the screen. "You should be proud, Winger. They're right about the quality. I especially like where you tried to add code you didn't think we'd see." He spun around so quick that the people nearest him stumbled back to get out of the way. "I can tell by the surprise on your face that you really thought you'd get away with it. I'm particularly disappointed in you, Cobb." In a fluid movement Westside turned away from me, pulled his gun and shot her at point-blank range.

Screams filled the room. Split Screen flinched. Wildcat turned a disturbing shade of gray.

Cobb dropped to the floor.

Westside spun around and held the gun on me. "Quite clever how you were going to attempt to hijack and destroy every computer in our network. You almost got away with it. Two lines of code looked out of place, and it had been bothering me in the last review. I just figured it out."

Fuck.

"I wish I could've convinced you to be on our side," Westside continued. "Now you can watch us succeed knowing you failed." He waved over one of the guards. "Don't let him move."

The guard trained his gun on me.

I didn't need to know the outcome.

Time to make the last move.

I pulled up the menu on the contact lenses and activated the pulse along with the order for the bots to attack the servers.

"Five," my phone said.

No! I hadn't disabled the audible countdown.

"Four."

"What's that?" Westside looked up from the monitor.

"Three."

"What did you do?" Westside asked, anger and panic tinged his voice.

"It's his phone," Cornerstone said from my desk.

"Two."

He grabbed a keyboard and drove the corner of it into the phone.

"One." The sound warbled.

Cornerstone looked up to Westside. "The screen's dark."

The green dot was gone. He'd hit the phone just right.

Sparks flew from the computers and lights. People yelped as phones crackled in their pockets. My phone might not have pulsed, but Split Screen's did.

I put my hands over my head as more electronics snapped across the room.

"You...." Westside howled, and he charged me. The room was in chaos as people moved away from anything electrical. Some small fires broke out.

Westside barreled into me but not before I got into a crouched position to take his blow. We went to the ground.

The lights went out.

Westside's fist connected with my jaw. He had me pinned.

People scrambled to get out of the room.

He tried to get another blow in, but I blocked him. I bucked, threw him off balance, and used the opportunity to get off a couple of punches of my own.

The building rocked with an explosion. What the hell was that? I hadn't expected anything to blow up.

More screams in the hallway.

Another, smaller, explosion went off. The building creaked.

"The floor's gonna give!" Split Screen shouted.

Westside got to his feet and headed for the door. His personal safety must be more important than beating me.

Part of the ceiling came down, and I heard a cry for help.

Split Screen.

I couldn't see her. Dust and smoke filled the room.

Creaks sounded all around. The building wouldn't last much longer.

"Winger?" Split Screen's voice again, weaker. "Are you here?"

"Yes."

I dropped to my knees. She struggled, trapped under rubble a few feet away.

I crawled to her and one leg was covered in heavy debris.

"I think it's broken," she said. "Maybe you should go before this gets worse." She sounded bizarrely calm.

"No," I said firmly. "We go together."

I wouldn't leave anyone else behind.

I moved, staying low, and worked to uncover her leg. I heard more coughing and turned to find Cornerstone.

"Let me help?" He started moving ceiling supports.

In no time we had her free and supported between us.

"Too much smoke. Where should we go?" Cornerstone said, sounding panicked as we got out of the room.

"There's only the one staircase so it's the only option."

He didn't question that.

The narrow staircase was a challenge, but we made it. On the first floor, we headed toward the front door. Sirens blared, and red lights flashed as people scrambled out the door.

We were blown forward, off our feet, by another explosion. As we hit the ground, everything got fuzzy.

THIRTY-ONE

Where was I?

This didn't look like any hospital room I'd ever seen. No window. No tray table to go over the bed. The TV sat on top of a filing cabinet instead of bolted to the wall. It played *Big Hero Six* and that made me smile.

I lay in a hospital bed, though, and an IV pumped fluid into my arm. A heart monitor beeped from behind.

I could move. Everything hurt, but it was manageable. Nothing seemed broken. I peered under the sheet. I was in boxers with the monitor leads contacted to my chest.

I fought going back to sleep. I had a lot of questions....

I gently shifted and felt a phone under my hand. Strange. I pulled it out. It wasn't mine.

As I tilted it toward me, a message flashed on the screen.

Great that you're awake. Text back. D-Man.

Thank God.

I quaked hard as a jumble of emotions crashed over me.

Was it over?

I tapped the screen and had a hard time seeing to type as tears filled my eyes.

The door sprang open, and Eddie ran in.

"Thank God. They kept saying you were okay, but I couldn't be sure."

"Eddie, my God. How are you here?"

He grabbed my hand, which was really all he could get to with the bed rails up. I wanted more, but for now this was amazing.

I couldn't stop the tears flowing—so much happiness knowing I was around friends.

"D-Man will be here in a minute, and the doctor's on the way to check you over."

He kissed my hand multiple times between each word. I tried to sit up, and he pushed buttons on the bed rail to raise the bed so I didn't have to move. Once upright, he dropped the rail and I pulled on his hand to bring him close for a proper kiss on the lips.

That calmed me more than expected.

"Is it over?" I asked when we separated.

"Excuse me, I'm sorry." The doctor appeared in the door. "I was very glad to hear you're awake, Winger. It's been thirty-six hours since you were brought in and while the tests looked good, it was still a long time to be out. If you don't mind...?" She looked to Eddie.

"I'd like to stay if that's okay."

"Of course. I just need room to get around the bed."

Eddie nodded and took a few steps back.

"I'm Montgomery," the doctor said. "How do you feel?" She started the tests with blood pressure.

"I hurt... all over. And tired."

She nodded as she moved on from blood pressure to

checking pupils, listening to my chest. The emotional outburst didn't stop, and I wept while she worked.

Coach came in and smiled as we locked eyes. "Winger, it's good to see your eyes open. The doctors kept saying you were fine, but—"

"I told him the same thing," Eddie chimed in.

"There are people who really want to see you." Coach held up his phone and looked at the screen. "Snowbird, Defender, I've got Winger here along with a civilian and Montgomery."

He turned the phone, so it was widescreen and Mom and Dad filled the screen. I didn't care about the louder sobs.

Montgomery must've recognized the importance of the reunion because she stepped back. Coach tried to put the phone in my hands, but I shook too much, so he held it.

My parents weren't in much better condition. I couldn't tell who held the phone, but it shook on their side, and they were both crying. Dad put his hand up on the camera for the virtual hug while we couldn't talk. Eddie circled around to the other side of the bed and let me squeeze his hand tight.

"Where are you guys?" I finally squeaked out.

"Toronto," Dad said. "I just got here last night to meet up with Snowbird. We'll be to you within the next four hours."

Another emotional tidal wave rolled over me, and I clamped down on Eddie's hand tighter while Coach put his free hand on my shoulder.

"And where am I?" I looked between the screen, Eddie, and Coach.

"This is Hanscom Air Force Base," Coach said. "We're about half an hour outside Boston."

I nodded. I had a rough idea where the base was.

"If I could interrupt for a moment," Montgomery said. "I'm sorry. Let me update you, and then you can continue. Believe me, I know how intense the last few days have been." She paused for a reassuring smile. "Winger, your vitals are good. I want to do another CT scan now that you're awake. If that's clear, we'll get you discharged."

"D-Man, could you turn the phone to the doctor, please?" Mom said, and he did as asked. "You're sure? The explosion and everything?"

"I assure you, Snowbird, that we won't let him out unless we can give him a 100 percent clean bill of health."

"Thank you, Montgomery."

"I'll let the nurse know to have you sent for the scan as soon as you're done. If one of you"—she looked between Coach and Eddie—"can let him know so we can get that out of the way."

"Yes, ma'am," Coach said. "We'll handle that."

"I'll see you after the tests, Winger, to explain the results."

"Thank you," I said with a mostly even voice.

She departed, leaving the three of us with my parents on the phone.

"Did Westside get away? How's Split Screen?"

I had many questions, but I started there.

"The mission, or whatever that was, doesn't matter right now, Winger," Dad said. "All that matters is that you're okay."

I shook my head so vigorously that it hurt. "No. I have to know if they're gonna go after anybody else."

"Winger, it—"

"Westside was apprehended on site," Coach cut Dad off. "He was injured escaping the building and taken into custody along with a significant number of the people who worked there. There was so much chaos that people were either too injured or shaken to try to escape."

I looked at him and didn't know what to say.

"When Locksmith and I had to move, instead of heading farther away, we came much closer, moving into the hotel on the other side of the park from where you were. While we'd lost the ability to talk to you, we still had the security cameras and heard the plans for the test. I knew we had to support you since I had no doubt you had a plan. I chanced reaching out to an FBI contact, and she got a strike team mobilized. Oh, and Locksmith ended up finding Eddie because he disobeyed my orders and slipped out to get coffee. Eddie'd gotten away from his Dad and came back to help you."

Unbelievable. While things went to hell inside, these guys were preparing to storm in. And Eddie. Wow. He'd come for me. I looked up to him, and he gave a shy smile and squeezed my hand gently.

"And Split Screen?"

"Her leg sustained severe damage below the knee." He looked around and his brow furrowed. "She might lose it. She's incredibly strong, though. She's already working with Amp and Red Hat debriefing on what she knows and working through analysis of what was recovered from the building. She was moved to HQ in Austin this morning."

"I guess that's good." Even as the words came out, they seemed wrong. "I mean... I'm glad she's...." What were the words here? She might lose a leg, so she's far from okay. I closed my eyes to regroup and continued to cling to Eddie's hand.

"Winger," Mom said in her soothing mom voice, "you need to rest."

"She's right," Dad quickly added. "Your job is to recover."

"But if Split Screen—"

"I think you've got your orders, Winger." Eddie had a certain mischievous glint in his eye that I wasn't sure I liked. Did he enjoy using that name?

I couldn't rest until I asked the question that scared me most. "What about Shotgun and Doc?"

That haunted look crossed Coach's face again.

Dad looked to Mom and then back to the screen. I tried to brace myself. "There's still no word on Doc. But, Shotgun...."

"No," I said, quietly.

Eddie gasped.

My hand became a vise grip on Eddie's and I pulled him closer.

"I should've...."

"You did the right thing," Mom said, voice strained as she tried to keep it together. "We've seen... we know... you came home to a horrible scene and...."

I sobbed. I thought I had no more in me, but a torrent unleashed, even though a part of me knew this news was coming.

Eddie dropped the rail and sat down close. I got as close to him as I could with the stupid IV tubing restraining me. "I'm so sorry."

"You have to know how much he'd want you to be safe," Dad said.

"But he—" Words came out in fits and starts. "—needed me. I...."

"Your 911 call got the ambulance there," Dad said. "His injuries were too severe. Even if you'd stayed, he wouldn't have—"

"Did I stop it?" I shouted. Eddie flinched, but didn't let me go. "Did the test...?"

"Oh, Th—" Mom caught herself before she said my name. "You prevented the test. The building is mostly rubble, and from what Amp says, they didn't even have the opportunity to start the test before all hell broke loose. And, with the agent list Split Screen recovered, we're picking up Blackbird agents around the world who had a major hand in the scheme. Locksmith's help was also invaluable. With the network map that he had saved separately, it allowed us to move on a number of locations where we found destroyed equipment."

Dad picked up. "It's not clear if Blackbird is fully dismantled, but you dealt them a major blow in terms of infrastructure and personnel."

I nodded. I'd done what I needed to. I relaxed and dropped my head against Eddie's shoulder.

"Winger?" Dad finally asked when no one had said anything for a while.

Another mission completed. Once again barely avoiding disaster.

"I'm sorry," I whispered. I looked back at the phone screen and their concerned faces stared back at me.

"For what?" Dad asked.

"All of it. None of it?" I struggled to sit up. "I don't know. It was all so messed-up. Some of it still is. What about Shotgun? Doc? Mitch? My God. Mitch has no idea about me. About Eddie. Coach. If we're okay. What have I done?"

"You did absolutely the best you could," Mom said. Tears ran down her face and I wanted to hug her. "The people working with Mitch say he's still shaken but okay. He hasn't been back to school yet, but he's physically fine with his minor injuries healing. Since the building explosion story was on TV, he's trying to find you and us. He wants to know that you're okay, but there's no information to give him right now. You should know, it was Mitch who told D-Man to find Locksmith."

I nodded. I did that way too much. My brain was scrambled with too much information so it was all I could do sometimes. But way to go Mitch.

"Of course, we need to figure out what the official story is before he can know anything," Dad added.

We were quiet for a moment. Eddie's hand soothingly rubbed over my head.

"Do you think we could talk to Winger alone for a few minutes?" Mom asked.

"You gonna be okay?" Eddie asked.

I pulled back a little and nodded weakly, trying to be strong. I wasn't sure I would be.

He lightly kissed my forehead before he stood. I wiped a hand across my face, trying to dry it. It didn't seem possible I could get it so wet from crying. Coach handed me some tissues from the side table.

"When you're done, you can text us on this phone." Coach held up the phone I'd initially contacted him on.

"Thanks."

He put the phone Mom and Dad were on in my hand and I kept it steady. Eddie kissed me one more time before he and Coach stepped out.

"Sorry about that," I said, wiping at my eyes more with a Kleenex.

"Don't be," Dad said. "We'd be worried if you weren't crying. You've been through a lot."

"I think we all have."

They nodded, and Mom pulled Dad a little closer.

"Can I ask what's going on with Eddie?" Mom said. "D-

Man says you two found him during Mitch's rescue. Apparently, he helped you too. Is he trustworthy?"

"I trust him." Mom's eyes narrowed a bit and her mouth went to a straight line. She didn't like this. "He said he was forced by his father. The last time I saw him before today he was being taken away, and he suspected that his father might kill him."

"He's in TOS custody," Dad said. "We're being cautious but giving him some leeway, like being able to see you. He's cooperated with all that we've asked, and he helped D-Man secure the scene at the building. But...." Dad hesitated.

"He got me through rough days," I said in the pause Dad left. "He's been through a lot too. He needs our help."

They traded a look I couldn't quite read. I couldn't blame them for not liking what I said. But I couldn't deny how crazy happy it made me when Eddie came through the door first and how he held me as I heard the worst possible news about John.

I yawned twice, pretty big. I quickly brought a hand to my mouth to cover it.

"Sorry. That snuck up on me."

That got a half smile out of Mom. "It's okay. We'll let you go. Call the nurse, get the test done, and rest. We'll be there soon."

"Do what your mom says." Dad winked at her, and she nudged him. Dad made a fist and bumped the camera, but before I could return it, Mom pushed his fist out of the way, so she could do it too. She never did that, and it sent all the warm feels through me. I bumped twice back—once for each of them.

"I love you guys."

"We love you too," Mom said.

"Can't wait to see you," Dad added.

The screen went dark as they disconnected.

Thank God they were safe and on the way.

I texted on the other phone that I could go for the scan. I missed the whole thing, though, because I was asleep before anyone came to get me.

THIRTY-TWO

I woke up a couple of hours later to find out the scans were okay and I could be discharged.

I got to go to another room that was clearly thrown together quickly to be as comfortable as possible. It looked like a garage sale had been raided because nothing matched, but since it was a safe place to be, I was okay with that.

Eddie had the room next door. While he technically had the designation of detainee, he had a similar room to mine, and he told me we had free rein in the hallway. A break room across the hall had a small kitchen with a fridge, microwave, a couple of tables, and a couch that had certainly seen better days given the slight sag in the middle. We wouldn't cook a gourmet meal, but there was a vast array of takeout to order, and we could eat together.

Even though I wasn't detained like Eddie, apparently I couldn't leave this hallway either, because they were keeping me out of sight. Only a handful of people knew I was on the base.

Coach had more freedom and thankfully went shopping at some point. He bought Eddie and me fresh clothes—

all the basics from underwear and socks to jeans, T-shirts, and hoodies.

It felt great to get a shower, do some basic warm-up stretches to loosen up, and put on clean clothes.

My stuff was effectively gone. Nothing from my backpack could be recovered from the building. No one had been back to the hotel to recover the few things that I had there and it had been decided to abandon those. As for the stuff at home, I suspected I'd never see it again. It probably didn't even matter.

Eddie, Coach, and I met up in the kitchen for a snack because I wanted food. My parents, meanwhile, had landed and were due any minute, and I couldn't wait.

"I didn't even ask what happened with D... um, Locksmith?" It felt odd to call him that, but codenames were all we used here. Only Eddie was exempt.

Coach nodded as he finished chewing one of the chicken tenders. "That kid's amazing. His skills remind me of yours. Based on the debrief I'd seen after the work you did with him before, I wasn't sure he'd be able to handle it, but he came through like a champ. He'd be a real asset to TOS if he's at all interested."

Dean had been so jittery with what had gone down at the computer science fair. This time, though, he was mostly behind a keyboard and not threatened by a bunch of gun-wielding men. I needed to thank him because I was sure this would've ended much differently without him.

"Who'd have thought saving him from a bully would end up like this." Eddie looked to me. "But still bizarre after all this time that...." Eddie trailed off a lot this morning. He kept saying nothing was wrong, but I knew his distracted habits and leaving incomplete thoughts was one of them. He chalked it up to being wiped out after everything, and I related to that. I wanted him to say what was on his mind, though.

The door opened and the MP who guarded our hall stood aside to allow my parents in. Questions for Eddie would have to wait.

It was just like a movie as I jumped from the table, ignoring any soreness, and ran for them. They both opened their arms, and I crashed in between them so we ended up in a three-way hug. There were "so good to see you" and "love yous" all around.

Once I had hold of them, I couldn't bring myself to let go and the longer we embraced, the more I quaked. I teetered on the edge of breaking down, yet I didn't because with them here it meant the worst was over. No matter what happened next, we'd be in it together.

John....

I had to get used to the fact he wouldn't be in any more reunions.

Mom and Dad didn't let me go. If anything, they held me tighter until I could finally step back. They looked tired but okay.

"Snowbird, Defender, it's good to see you," Coach said from behind us. I hadn't even heard him get up from the table.

Dad started with a handshake but then pulled Coach into a hug. Mom did the same as soon as Dad stepped back. I looked to the table, but Eddie was gone.

Weird.

"Thanks for watching out for him." Mom looked to me with still glassy eyes. "He's good at what he does, but I'm glad he wasn't alone all the time."

"It goes without saying," Coach said, "you should be very proud. He was extraordinary." He clapped me gently on the shoulders. "I'll give you three some privacy. They've made up a room for you here as well. Some place to stay until there's a decision on what to do next."

They nodded, and I suspected they already had a plan.

"Where'd Eddie go?"

"Back to his room?" Coach continued quietly. "He's worried about what comes next. He'd actually thanked me earlier for not just shooting him. I don't know why he'd think I'd do that without provocation."

Why hadn't he told me he felt that way? I hope it was clear to TOS how much he'd helped.

"We'll talk about it. We've been discussing him, among other things, on the flight," Mom said.

Coach nodded. "I'll be down the hall if you need me." He headed out without another word.

Dad put his arm around me. "In case it wasn't clear, we are very proud of you. You stopped something that would've been horrific. We've reviewed Split Screen's debriefing. You made great decisions."

"Thanks. I hoped for the best, since I was making it all up." I shrugged, uncomfortable.

"Why don't we sit?" Mom asked.

A knock at the door interrupted us, and the guard came in with three bags of food. I smelled garlic!

"We didn't know you already had food so we had them order some when we arrived. We're famished from the trip and figured you could eat too."

"I'm crazy hungry all the time so the more the better. Like my body is making up for those days."

Dad took the food to the table and unpacked it. I went to the fridge and got waters and Cokes for them and my Dr Pepper.

"I see at least they found you some Dr Pepper," Mom said, serving food onto the plastic plates. "That's good."

"Yeah. D-Man made sure. I think he made it pretty clear that it would keep me happy. Even Blackbird had it, which was a little weird."

"Let's sit on the couch," Dad said. "I've had enough of uncomfortable chairs for a while."

I was good wherever because they were here. I'd sit on the floor if they wanted to. They took either end of the couch, and I dropped in between them. It was perfect.

"There's so much to discuss," Dad said. "Where do you want to start? The official debrief won't happen until the three of us get to HQ. We'll fly before dawn tomorrow."

"What's left? Blackbird made it sound like they'd decimated TOS."

They traded a brief look of worry—one I suspected I'd see a lot in the coming weeks. I knew they'd tell me what my clearance allowed.

"HQ got hit hard," he said. "A lot of people died there. Since they got the list, they were able to get to even remote embedded agents. Some avoided them, while others were captured, injured, or killed. Agents who were deployed, like me, didn't get caught, most likely because we were harder to get to."

"You should know," Mom said, sounding grave, "that Raptor was killed at HQ. Red Hat is temporary director. It's not clear who'll fill that role permanently."

The air felt like it got sucked out of my lungs. Could TOS survive without the leader at the helm?

A knock at the door interrupted, and Dad called out, "Come in."

"Sorry to interrupt," Coach said, entering with a package. "This is for Winger. It arrived by courier."

He handed over the package, and it made me tear up for a moment. The shape of the box told me that this was electronics, likely a laptop and phone. Doc usually sent them. Who sent this one?

"Thanks," I said quietly.

"You're welcome. Figured you'd want to get online. I'll let you all get back to the catch-up." He left and closed the door behind him.

"Still nothing about Doc?" I asked.

They both shook their head, and my mind flashed on the last moments I'd seen him.

"And what's this about Austin?"

"Austin is the disaster recovery point. They're moving people and tech to that facility. That's where we'll be going. I'm sure you've got emails about it."

It was a lot to take in and it only scratched the surface of my questions. How could they be so calm?

If they'd been through anything like this, they'd never told me about it. I wish they could share more of their mission experiences to help me understand how I should react to everything.

"What's gonna happen with Eddie?"

That stumbled out of my mouth before I could catch it. Of everything that needed to be discussed that probably ranked pretty low for them, but it mattered a lot to me.

Mom sighed. Had she meant to sound so exasperated? "I don't know. We haven't focused on that. It's been more about getting TOS back up in a secure fashion as quickly as possible."

"Maybe we should spend a little more time there," Dad said, looking past me toward Mom. "There are considerations beyond any mission where he's concerned."

"He helped while I was on site." I cringed at how

overeager that sounded not to mention that I repeated what they already knew.

"We've read his initial debrief." Dad ran his hand through his hair and Mom looked flustered. "We don't have answers... from either an agency point of view or as your parents. He came after you personally and professionally. Even if the agency decides to clear him, I don't know if I can."

"We don't have to figure it all out right now," Mom said. "It's going to be a while before we get back any sort of normalcy."

They clearly knew things I didn't. I wasn't surprised. After all, I'd been cut off for nearly a week. That statement about normal, though; she tried to make it sound like it was nothing.

"We're not going back home, are we? Not ever." No reason to not let them know I'd already thought of that.

"No," Dad said. He didn't like talking about it either. "Too much has been breached. They gave us the option after New York, but I can't imagine they will this time."

I stood up quick. The sudden movement made my muscles scream.

I desperately wanted a window to look out. I settled for going back to the food and picked up a breadstick to nibble on. I didn't need to turn around to know they watched me closely.

"We're going to be split up?" I asked.

I kept my distance, but I turned to face them.

"We're not sure what the agency will want and how much input they'll take from us," Mom said.

"I don't want you guys to be separated." I took a big bite out of the breadstick to keep me from having to talk again because emotions rose fast. I would hate myself if something I'd done forced them apart. Despite what they've always said, I had little doubt that the blame was mine for the breach in our cover.

"We'll see. There's a lot that goes into dealing with this kind of thing."

The breadstick shook in my hand, and I clamped down on a chair back trying to force myself to calm down. I'd hoped they'd know what would come next. They didn't, and that left me unsure and a little bit scared.

"All we can do is tell you that it will all get worked out." Mom got up and came toward me.

"Tomorrow," Dad added as he followed, "we'll all go to Austin and start to figure out the future."

"Does Eddie come with us?"

Dad looked annoyed, but he swallowed that fairly quickly before he spoke. "Yes. The rest of his debrief will be there. D-Man goes back to Boston. He'll be there through the end of the school year as a way to keep an eye on Mitch. His exposure is fairly limited, but once the season's done, he'll leave and be reassigned."

I leaned against Dad's shoulder and reached out and took Mom's hand.

At least we'd face whatever came next together.

THIRTY-THREE

I SPENT a quiet evening with my parents, which included burgers from a local place that the people on base swore by. Eddie kept his distance. Coach let us have space too.

We flew out at the way too early time of 4:30 and arrived in Austin four hours later. I tried to sleep on the flight, but it came in fits and starts thanks to the dreams.

I tried to get in touch with Shields because if ever there was a time to talk to my counselor this was it. All those calls went to voicemail, and Mom and Dad didn't know her status. They offered to talk about whatever I wanted, but there were things I couldn't bring myself to talk to them about. I needed to come to terms with the emotions, the fear, the nightmares, and everything else.

We landed in Austin at a private airstrip and took a black SUV with tinted windows to a building on the outskirts of the city. It was part of an office park. The signage outside read Credit Dauphine. The windows were all heavily tinted, no doubt allowing people to look out but none to look in. We drove into a loading dock and didn't get out of the car until the door was down.

I couldn't get out fast enough. Lorenzo came up behind Red Hat, a.k.a. Joanna, to greet us. Another man stood with them, but I didn't recognize him.

All decorum went out the window as I sprinted to him. I stopped short, though, as I saw a cane in his left hand, the angry bright purple bruise across his face, and patch over his left eye.

"Winger, my God, it's good to see you. Bring it in." He held out his arms, lifting the cane off the ground. I couldn't resist stepping into the hug, but I kept my hold light... at least until he wrapped his arms around me tight. I carefully squeezed more. Thank God for another reunion.

I stayed in the hug until he let me go. He wobbled a little, and I steadied him until he got the cane set. What the hell had they done to him? Despite his appearance, he smiled, and his one eye sparkled with happiness.

"Doc, Jesus."

"Yeah. I wasn't going down without a major fight. I'm sorry I couldn't get in touch with you sooner. I only got here about ninety minutes ago and—"

"It's my fault," Red Hat said. "We kept his arrival under wraps."

Red Hat looked beyond haggard. I'd seen her on and off during missions, and she usually looked calm and put together. Instead of the smart suit she usually wore, she was dressed down in jeans and a sweater. Yes, TOS maintained a casual dress code, but I'd never seen her looking anything other than CEO impeccable. I wondered what she'd gone through.

"Snowbird, Defender, good to have you here." They all shook hands and even embraced briefly. "We've got a lot to talk about."

I looked for Eddie because I wanted to introduce him to Lorenzo, but he stood by the car.

"Hemingway," Joanna said to the previously unknown person, "please show Mr. Cochrane to his room and make sure he's comfortable but kept under guard."

"Yes, ma'am." I watched as he approached Eddie and directed him to walk ahead.

"Theo?" Eddie stopped next to me and looked more scared than I'd ever seen.

"I'll come see you later. You're safe. I promise." Hopefully I wasn't making a promise I couldn't see through.

He nodded and started walking again with Hemingway next to him, hand on his forearm.

"Snowbird, Defender if we could meet now, I'd appreciate it. Winger, you'll start with Doc, and we'll meet later."

"Understood," I said.

"The damage reports are being collated so we can prioritize what needs to be done," Lorenzo said. "I can review with you what we already know."

Joanna gestured to my parents, and they went off together.

"How are you doing, Winger?" Lorenzo asked when we were alone.

It was weird to be called by codename at headquarters. That hadn't been typical before.

"Overall, I guess good. At least as good as could be expected."

He turned and started to walk, and I fell in next to him. He was slow, and I adjusted to keep us even.

"What about you? You look...." Why did I say that? He knew how bad he looked. What kind of friend was I?

"You can say it," he said, looking my direction with a smirk. "I look like I lost a round or two to an MMA fighter."

"Yeah, that works." A small chuckle escaped me, and he laughed too.

"It's good to laugh about it. I hurt all over." He stopped for a second, and his expression clouded over. "They beat me pretty bad and messed up my leg. Potentially permanent nerve damage." He stopped, but I knew we needed to finish.

"And the...."

"They took it. They got tired of trying to hold my eyelids open enough to get the scan to work. Of course once it was out, it didn't work anyway."

I couldn't hold in a gasp. As bad as it'd been for me, Lorenzo got hit much worse.

"I'm lucky all of it went down in headquarters. Once some of our people returned, they found me and.... Well... I don't like to think about how it might have gone if they hadn't shown up when they did."

I gently put my hand on his shoulder and gave the faintest of squeezes.

"Why aren't you recovering somewhere?"

"There's a lot to do. And we lost a lot of the IT folks at HQ. Believe it or not, I'm lucky."

My God. If he was lucky....

"I need to ask you something that you can say no to. But you're my first choice. I know you turned this down before, but we... I... really need you, even if it's for a short time." What had him nervous? Lorenzo didn't usually stumble over his words. "Can you be my number two? You're one of the only people who has an extensive knowledge of our systems and can start work immediately."

Given what I already knew from my parents, it wasn't like I would go back to school or a regular life anytime soon, so it was easy to say yes this time.

The rest of the day was split up between debriefings and working with Lorenzo and the tech team who were onsite. The number of team members grew throughout the day as people came in from remote locations.

Despite the damage to IT, it felt good getting in with a team I trusted to figure out how to quickly reassemble the infrastructure while also making plans to make it more resilient than ever.

I STOOD in front of the mirror, dread spreading through my chest. I'd only put on the black pants so far and couldn't push myself to finish.

With everything going on, I don't know who found the time to get me a suit. It seemed unimportant. Yet I was glad to have it. John wouldn't have cared if I'd shown up in jeans and a sweatshirt, but he deserved more than that.

There'd been memorials for the past few days. Joanna didn't allow John's to be scheduled until Mom, Dad, and I were here.

John's actual funeral was today too. His parents still lived in Boise, where he'd grown up, so it would take place there. None of us could go, although we wanted to.

Technically I was still missing, and my parents were working to get information on me. Mom did talk to John's parents, though, and sent condolences. We knew his mom and dad. They'd visited him a couple of times in Boston, and we'd see them when they were in town. Like Mom, John had FBI credentials, so it helped their cover had them as colleagues.

TOS also made sure, behind-the-scenes, that all the funeral expenses were covered.

I needed to finish.

The first time I'd worn a suit I was eight. To that point I lived in jeans or shorts and T-shirts—not too much different from today. We'd been invited to a baptism, and Mom said that I had to look nice—and that didn't mean wearing my new Red Wings tee.

John explained that dressing up was something we did sometimes to honor a special moment. I went along with it. If Mom and John thought it was important, it must be.

Mitch went to that baptism too and we griped throughout that afternoon even as our parents fawned over how grown-up we looked.

I slipped on the shirt—also black—and slowly buttoned it. My hands shook, making it difficult at times to get the buttons through the holes.

I had to get through this. John deserved my best.

I'd been told repeatedly that I'd done all I could. Done what was important by following his order.

The information offered no comfort.

Tears were on the verge of spilling over but didn't quite come, and the longer they didn't, the closer I got to flying apart at the seams.

Keys's death, more than six months ago now, had rocked my world. She'd been a colleague, mentor, and friend. While John was all those things, he was family above all else. We may have called him *uncle*, but he was everything from stand-in parent to older brother.

I tucked in the shirt, zipped, buttoned, and belted the pants.

Suits weren't my favorite thing, but I was used to it. The team wore them every week to school on game day.

The tie....

Dad wasn't home the first time I had to wear a suit for school—freshman year, first game. He was due at the game, but his flight had been delayed so he wasn't around that morning. We'd bought the suit before he'd left, and he taught me how to tie the tie.

At least we thought he had.

I couldn't do it that morning—the ends wouldn't balance out.

I tore into the kitchen for help because I didn't want to be late for carpool. John calmed me down, took me to the mirror in the hall, and showed me. We did it a few times to make sure I could do it myself.

Crisis averted.

I needed his steady hands because my shaking made it difficult.

A soft knock at the door startled me.

Opening it I found Dad.

"Are you—"

I stood with the tie in my right hand, looking at him, tears rolling down my cheeks. I fought the urge to wipe them with the tie.

"We got this," he said, coming in and closing the door.

He hugged me, and I nodded against his shoulder, trying to rein in the emotions.

I stepped back and wordlessly handed him the tie. He flipped up the shirt collar, and within a minute he had the stupid tie in place.

I grabbed the jacket, but Dad put his hand out and stopped me from putting it on.

"You have to know," he said, voice sounding strained, "that there's no doubt John was so proud of you."

I nodded. I'd done what I needed to. He'd been part of my training, so he was one of the reasons I got through.

"He'll be a part of everything you do, guiding the choices you make, watching over you."

I hoped so.

"Thanks, Dad." I smiled weakly.

We hugged again, and I managed to keep it together.

He took the jacket from me and held it out for me to slip into.

"Let's go," I said.

THE ROOM WAS JAMMED to an almost uncomfortable extent. John had been with TOS for nearly fifteen years and while most of that time had been working with my parents, he'd formed a lot of close connections.

Mom clutched a Kleenex in her hand and used it often. I'd never seen her like this. My parents never hesitated to show emotion, and they'd passed that on to me. Mom, however, typically held it together. Dad fared only slightly better as he held on to both of us—one hand on my shoulder and his other holding Mom's. We stayed together and talked with the people who came up to us before the service began. No one talked specifically about how John died, and I appreciated that because I replayed that scene too often already. The comments focused on how great he'd been to work with and what a good friend he'd been.

I really wanted Eddie here with me. Holding his hand would've been a huge comfort, but he'd been in detention since we'd arrived. He spent most of his time debriefing, and we'd only been allowed to see each other for a few moments before his first interview. I wouldn't see him again until the interviews were done. Winger understood why; Theo wanted to see his boyfriend again.

"Winger, look who's here." Lorenzo approached with someone I'd indeed been eager to talk to—Shields.

"Winger, I'm sorry I haven't been available the last couple of days. It's been…."

I held up a hand. "It's okay. I'm so glad you're safe." Seeing her added to the feelings that created a whirlpool in my soul that threatened to overtake me. I selfishly hoped we'd be able to have a long talk today because I had so much to say.

"I'm so sorry for your loss with Shotgun. I've blocked out my afternoon, so you and I can talk if Doc and Red Hat can spare you."

I darted my eyes toward Lorenzo, and he nodded. "I've already talked to Red Hat. Take whatever time you need."

Wish granted.

"Good," she said with a concerned smile.

"Thanks," I said, voice broken.

A minister called us together. He stood at a podium as everyone took seats—this room normally had a conference table in it, but it had been used for many gatherings like this one and had rows of chairs.

Pastor Stein had been well briefed on what John did and what he meant to people. His words to us, who he'd referred to as John's second family, were more comforting than I'd expected. They reinforced what Dad had said earlier—that he'd always be near.

Mom, Dad, and I wanted to speak. In fact we would be the only ones other than Red Hat, who was paying respects on behalf of the agency. Mom and Dad said I wasn't obligated to, but there was no way I could stay quiet. John meant a lot, and I needed the moment to say goodbye.

I sat next to my parents. They'd spoken without anything written, and I hadn't put anything on paper either, but I wished I had. When Dad finished and returned to his seat, I suddenly worried I couldn't put into words what John meant to me.

At the podium, I looked at the people assembled, but every time I opened my mouth, I didn't know where to begin. As I studied my shoes for inspiration, Dad came back to the podium and put his hand on my shoulder. I met his gaze, and he gave a slight nod—it said everything. I could either go on or step away, and it would be okay. My nod sent him back to his seat. I had to do this.

"Shotgun has been part of my life for almost as long as I can remember," I said, shakily. "For a long time, I considered him to be my uncle—my mom's brother. He was around when my parents weren't. Later he became a trusted colleague, and on more than one occasion, he and I worked together to help agents in the field who needed a little extra tech support."

I took a deep breath to try and steady myself, so I could speak clearly. "My favorite times working with him when I started out focused on simple tasks. We'd huddle around the computers in my room and—this might be breaking usual protocol—we'd make a video game out of it. We'd have popcorn and snacks while I'd hack into security systems or remotely open locks while he'd relay information. We knew it was serious business, but he made it more interesting for a twelve-year-old. He never stopped bringing popcorn anytime we worked in front of my computers.

"I owe Shotgun—"

A sob leapt out, stepping on the words I wanted to say. I gripped the sides of the podium and focused on my parents.

While their eyes were moist, they beamed so much love in my direction it bolstered me to continue.

"I owe Shotgun my life. I'll never forget that. But I'll try to focus more on the good times when he was simply a member of the family. The guy who often came to my hockey games, joined us for family dinners, tried desperately to get me to like literature, and who was always there when my parents couldn't be.

"I've thought a lot the past few days about one of his favorite novels—one I hated reading for school until he showed me how a story set over one hundred years ago was relevant to today. I got an A on my paper about *Ragtime*, and the book's become one of my favorites. He liked a lot of passages in that book—but one in particular from the end he loved because of the closure it brought: 'And by that time the era of Ragtime had run out....' Shotgun, may you rest in peace. While our era has ended, I'll do my best to live up to the chance that you've given me to create more history."

I returned to my seat next to Mom, who pressed more tissues into my hand that I immediately put to use. She patted my knee, and I resisted the urge to lay my head against her shoulder. It didn't seem proper in this setting.

After a final prayer from the minister, the service was over, and the gathering shifted into a wake. I hugged Mom and Dad and excused myself. I had to get out before the walls closed in.

John was gone.

It wasn't clear what would happen to me, Mom, Dad, and Eddie.

At least I was useful here. Lorenzo made that extremely clear.

In the hall I stood with my back to the wall, working to catch my breath and keep from freaking out.

"Winger?" Shields spoke in her usual soothing tone.

"Sorry." I looked to her. We usually talked by phone only sometimes using FaceTime or Skype. It'd been a while since I'd seen her kind, gentle eyes.

"Don't apologize. You can take only so much before you have to release what you're feeling. What you're going through is significant and uncharted for you."

"Do you think...?"

It wasn't the right time.

"What?" she asked when I didn't continue.

"Could we maybe talk now?" I blurted out. "I really don't think I can go back in there."

"Of course. Come on, I've got a temporary office."

I pushed off the wall just as Dad stepped into the hall. Was I letting him down, or John, by not being with everyone else?

I turned, crashed into Dad, and wrapped my arms around him. He embraced me tight. What did the people in the room think about what was happening through the open door? No one else was having a meltdown.

"I'm sorry. Sorry. Sorry. Sorry," I said, softer each time through tears that would not stop.

"Oh, Theo," he said... the first time anyone had said my actual name outside of our residence quarters since I arrived. "It's okay. It'll all be okay."

Dad's voice was calm. How could he be so calm?

The world had flown apart.

"Honey," Mom rubbed the small of my back below Dad's hug. "Come on. We've been here long enough."

"Come," Shields said. "We can all go talk."

I don't know how she had so much time, but we talked for hours. For a while Mom and Dad were with us, but then they left us alone. We took a few breaks along the way—

sometimes to let me recover from crying and sometimes just to get up, stretch, and get something to drink or go to the restroom. It was a weight off me getting to unload everything with Shields. We set it up, so I'd see her daily to talk about anything I needed to—that felt like one part of normalcy restored.

THIRTY-FIVE

I RELISHED BEING BACK on the ice. It'd only been thirteen days since the last practice with Mitch and the team, but it felt like an eternity. Even the massive layoff from the shoulder injury last season seemed less.

I probably called in every favor that I ever had with TOS, even ones I might've earned during the mission that had just occurred, to make this happen. I convinced everyone it was the right thing to do for a number of reasons. My parents, Shields, and Coach were accomplices.

It was nearly eleven at night, and the rink was deserted this late on a weeknight. My gear was still locked up in my locker because as far as anyone knew, I was still coming back to the team. Once I was done here, the gear would go back, exactly how I always placed it, and I'd never see it again.

I skated the perimeter of the rink, feeling the skates scrape against the ice and making the telltale sound I loved so much. My helmet was off, and the breeze that I kicked up ruffled my longer-than-usual hair.

I stopped and turned as the rink door's distinct *thunk* sounded.

"Theo!" Mitch looked to me from across the ice, holding his helmet and stick.

I skated over fast, stopping in front of him and spraying shaved ice onto his shins. We smiled and stared at each other.

I hoped he wasn't going to freak. I'd spent most of yesterday doing that while I talked to Shields about this.

"Coach said you were gonna be here, but I still didn't quite believe it. Are you okay? I kept hoping the news would mention something about you. I know the building you got me out of blew up the other day." I nodded. "Were you there?"

I nodded again. "I was, yeah. Got the job done."

His mouth hung open adding to his already confused look. "What was all that about?" he finally asked. "All Coach told me when he brought me home was that I couldn't tell anyone about you two, or Eddie, and to say that I couldn't identify any of the people who had me. Basically I had to say that they just let me go. The cops somehow accepted it."

"It's complicated. I can't tell you much."

"Are you like 007 or something? You seemed kinda badass showing up there."

I laughed, and it felt so good to do that with Mitch. "Come on, let's skate a little, and we'll talk."

He nodded, and we stopped at the bench, so he could put his helmet and stick down next to mine. We took off to skate at an easy pace around the outer perimeter of the oval.

"I like to think of myself more as Q than 007, but yeah, I've worked for an agency for a while now. That's really all I can tell you, and I probably shouldn't have said that. I'm breaking all kinds of procedure even being here. I had to come thank you. If you hadn't told Coach to talk to Dean, I honestly don't know if I'd have survived."

We built up speed, following one of our routine warm-ups. We fell into it without even talking about it.

"Look, let me say this to get it out of the way so we can have some fun here before I have to go." We didn't break stride as I talked. We'd done this for so many years that we had to go a lot faster before we couldn't talk. "As you can probably guess with all the secrecy, you can't tell anyone that you've seen me."

"Okay. Sure."

I started to say more but had to take a breath before I spoke. I'd thought a lot about how to tell Mitch what would happen next. I'd even practiced it in front of a mirror in the plane's bathroom during the trip up here. "Tomorrow it'll break in the news that I was found in the rubble of the building."

As we went around a curve behind a goal line, he kept looking to me and then back straight ahead. Ultimately, he stopped so hard that I had to turn back to get to him.

"What does that mean?"

"Theodore Reese will be declared dead tomorrow."

He looked on the verge of losing it. I wished I could've cushioned the blow somehow.

"What does it mean? Are your parents okay with this? Do they know?"

"They do. They helped me get permission to tell you. But, seriously, not a word—ever. It could be seriously bad." He nodded vigorously. "I've been an agent for six years now —mostly behind the computer, but more recently I've been out doing missions. I got into it because my parents were doing it."

"Damn, you think you know somebody." He laughed. I could tell he was trying to keep his shit together, but at least he could find a little humor.

"I'm sorry I had to hide stuff."

He made a *pfft* noise. "Please. I know how that secret identity stuff works." He took some easy strides, and we got back into the skating. "At least that explains some of the weirdness over the last year," he continued.

"For sure."

He looked to me as he kept his speed up. "So what happens to you?"

"It'll be like witness protection. New identity, new life, new everything."

"Wow," he said with reverence, like it was something cool. "So, I never see you again?"

I shook my head.

I'd suspected it would happen. I didn't want it, but there weren't other options at this point. New identities would keep everyone safe. I didn't have specifics on when the new IDs would be ready, but it would be soon.

"Oh man," he said with the sadness I dreaded hearing. "I thought we'd be those guys who stayed friends forever. You know, phone calls keeping up with our teams. Probably be godfathers to our kids. See each other at least a couple of times a year."

He sounded wistful, and it pulled at my heart since there was nothing I could do.

"I'm sorry, man. I wish it could be different."

"It'll be okay." He went faster, and I followed suit. "I know a spy. That's pretty cool." His mouth worked into one of his goofy smiles. Only Mitch could take something that shredded both of us and find any sort of silver lining. His glassy eyes betrayed how he really felt, though.

"Listen," I said, "this is gonna be sappy, but you need to know that you're an amazing friend. I hate that my work messed it all up. I can only hope that wherever I settle next, I end up with a friend as good as you. You set the bar super high."

Mitch caught my arm and brought us to an easy stop. "First of all, no one can be as awesome as me." His bravado made me smile. "Seriously, though, don't talk like that. This is hard enough."

I nodded and pulled him into an embrace. Hugging in hockey gear might not be easy with the extra padding, but we managed a pretty good one, and he slapped me on the back a couple of times.

"We have some time for a little one-on-one before you have to go?"

"Oh yeah. More people than you can imagine are watching right now to make sure that no one bothers us. Coach will let us know when we have to wrap up."

We headed for the bench to get our stuff.

"What happened...?"

"Go ahead, ask." He at least should ask even if I couldn't answer.

"What happened with Eddie? You haven't talked about him."

I considered what I could say. He'd seen Eddie so....

"You don't have to answer. I shouldn't have asked."

"I haven't seen him in a few days, but he's safe." I finally dove in.

"I don't know exactly what happened with you two but... will you get back with him?"

I appreciated how he jumped over agent stuff and went right to the heart of the matter.

I strapped my helmet on as I figured out what to say.

"You'll never know how fucked up it was. But, man, I need advice. I haven't gotten over him, and the time we spent together while I was in that building was pretty great, all things considered. But I have no idea if that's the right thing to do. I don't even know with the new identity if he and I would be allowed to be together."

He popped his helmet on, and I recognized his deep-in-thought expression. If he'd had a pencil in his hand, he would've been chewing on the eraser.

"There's so much I could say, but I'll go with this—follow your heart and keep yourself safe."

I managed to swallow my urge to weep at how earnest he was.

"That's perfect. My heart wants him bad."

"I think you've got your answer."

I grabbed my stick and passed Mitch his. I grabbed one of the pucks from the ledge and tossed it onto the ice.

"Full ice one-on-one, only posts count as goals."

"You're on," he said, and the competitive gleam in his eye fired me up. In that moment it was like the past two weeks hadn't happened.

SKATING with Mitch would be one of the things I missed most.

After the epic training camp we'd been to, our senior season was set up to be amazing. We'd both improved and were starting to show that in the preseason practices. Even our one-on-one game had changed as both of us seemed able to think a couple moves ahead. It made for a thrilling challenge.

I'd be able to follow Mitch and the team's season

online—if I could handle it. It would be tough watching and not being a part of it. Even when I was injured, I went to the games, supported the team. I'd be reduced to looking at stats and whatever highlight reels I could find online.

After Mitch made a particularly spectacular shot that ended with the loudest *plink* against the crossbar, I stopped, completely overwhelmed.

"Theo?" Mitch was next to me in a heartbeat, hand on my shoulder.

I shook my head. "I'm really gonna miss you." My voice faltered and cracked like when it had changed.

He simply nodded, and I brought my eyes up to meet his. I couldn't tell if he cried too or if it was sweat running down his face.

I slid the helmet off and used my jersey sleeve to wipe my eyes.

"Let's not do this now," Mitch said; his voice also cracked a bit. "We're wasting ice time."

I nodded and attempted a grin. I slid the helmet back on and skated quick to the rink corner where the puck had landed. I took a couple of strides with it before sending it hard to the other end of the rink. We both sprinted after it.

We played for nearly two hours with just a couple of water breaks. Coach banging on the Plexiglas signaled that our time was up.

"So this is it?" Mitch said after we'd changed. Neither of us spoke as we cleaned up and put gear away. I knew this wouldn't be easy, but it proved to be far more difficult. I wanted to take my jersey but couldn't. Owning anything from my past would be a risk—even if it was just packed in a box.

"Yeah. But, don't think I won't be watching, I'll know

how you're doing." I tried to smile. "Give Iris a big hug for me, even though she won't know it's from me."

"The biggest, man." He was just about to open the door to the locker room when he stopped and looked back to me. "I know you'll never do this, but know that if you need something, I'm here. I have no doubt you'll be able to find me, and if you ever need to, I got your back."

I stepped in and we hugged tight. "Thanks, Mitch. For everything."

We clapped each other a couple times and walked out to Coach.

"Mitch, you head out," he said, "and we'll leave after you're safe back home."

He nodded, and sadness clouded his face. "Thanks for helping set this up. His secrets are safe with me, I promise."

Coach nodded.

"Take care of yourself." I put out my fist and he bumped it before heading out the player exit.

THIRTY-SIX

THE MORNING I got back from skating with Mitch, I had a meeting with Mom, Dad, Joanna, and Lorenzo. From the time I got up I couldn't focus on anything other than trying to guess what I'd hear.

I went to the conference room with Lorenzo. His demeanor seemed to change from his usual even-keeled to cloudy. By the time we got there, he looked downright concerned. Granted, he was more difficult to read with the eye patch, which he was due to have for several more months.

Those missing from the meeting—Raptor and John—tugged at the wound that was still raw.

"Thanks for gathering first thing," Joanna said. "We wanted to brief you all on what we know currently about Blackbird and what's going to happen in the next few days." She looked to Lorenzo, who picked up the tablet in front of him to consult notes.

"The more we review the Blackbird network, the more we can validate the destruction is significant. We can't guarantee that it's complete, but we've recovered servers that were connected to the IP's we identified. In some cases we've been able to use the recovered units to access other areas of the network and disable additional machines. We'll never know if we got everything—much the same that Blackbird likely couldn't validate if they got our entire network."

Everyone around the table nodded as he put the tablet down. My code wiped out more than I'd expected. While Westside had said he'd found my code, he apparently had no time to remove it before I activated it.

"From a personnel standpoint," Dad said, "getting their list allowed us to round up a number of agents and struck deep into the heart of their leadership as well. We not only have their director but several of his top deputies. We had worldwide cooperation going after these targets to help bring an end to their reign of chaos. As for our own team, our losses were high, with 23 percent of our agents killed and another 6 percent injured but recovering. It's unknown currently if all of them will choose to return to work."

I hadn't heard these numbers for TOS losses and those tempered the good news about Blackbird.

"Winger, can you update on recovery? I know we're meeting on the rebuild later, but a high-level status now would be great."

I'd been asked by so many how we were doing that I could give a status report at any time.

"We've made significant strides in getting the global network back online and should be completed in the next twenty-four to thirty-six hours. Primary applications are already back online. We're having some trouble with the comm systems in Europe for reasons that we're still troubleshooting, and I don't have an ETA on that yet. We're also having lingering issues with the tracker system in China,

Australia, and areas of Japan. We've got people on the ground looking at that, particularly in China."

I caught Dad's smile out of the corner of my eye. I felt better today than I had in some time. Seeing Mitch, alongside all the discussion I'd had with Shields and my parents since John's funeral, helped reduce my stress. Working on the systems recovery helped too, since I enjoyed the work. Things were far from perfect, but at least there were moments I could breathe without worrying about what would happen next.

"That's very good progress." Red Hat looked pleased as she typed notes into her tablet.

"From the IT staffing standpoint," Lorenzo said, "we've got several excellent candidates in the pipeline, and I've made some hires. A couple of them will be here later today so we can get them to work. We're probably still a good sixty days away from being back to where we were. Our disaster recovery protocols need a full review, and we'll be updating those starting next week."

Joanna nodded, made a few more notes, and then closed the cover on her tablet. "Winger, you played a central role in thwarting Blackbird's plan, and getting us back up and running with great speed. You've also borne some of the worst fallout. I want to talk about what happens from here. Your parents are going to go to Boston as soon as we're done here. They'll play the role of the grieving parents and in short order they'll sell the house and move."

"You'll be glad to know the agency isn't splitting us up," Mom said. "But, after a few months, Victor and Katherine Reese will quietly disappear and we'll take on new identities."

I let go a sigh of relief.

"I plan to continue my usual role here," Dad said,

"going on missions as needed. In the short term, though, I'll be working more domestically while the team is rebuilt." Good. Dad loved fieldwork. "Your mom on the other hand has some big news."

Dad looked so proud as a wide smile spread across his face.

"Red Hat asked me to take over the director role stepping into Raptor's shoes. I've excepted the role effective immediately."

No wonder Dad smiled, and I couldn't hold mine back. Mom had done so much in the field and training new agents over the years that she'd be amazing at the job. In a very un-agent move, I got up, came behind her, and wrapped her in the biggest hug I could with her sitting in a chair.

"Congratulations. That's awesome." She put her hands on mine, and we held it for just a moment before I returned to my seat.

Everyone smiled, but suddenly it felt wrong to do that given the losses.

"I'm sorry," I said, reining myself in, "that may not have been the right reaction given what's brought you the promotion. But it's still cool that we'll be in such good hands."

"It's okay," Joanna said. "Snowbird's going to be great, and we shouldn't shun the opportunity to celebrate what we can given how we've suffered."

So Mom and Dad knew their future. "What's the plan for me?"

I looked between all of them unsure of where to look for the answer.

"You'll live and work here for at least the next six months. It's important to keep you out of sight." When Mom spoke, I couldn't decide if she was being director or Mom. "I know that's not exactly a fair request for a seventeen-year-old, but part of the time will be spent assessing how much risk Blackbird still poses and at the same time constructing your new identity. And, as the director of TOS, I want you here working alongside Doc and the team to make us better than before. Once the six months has passed, you can decide where you choose to live and what you do."

There were almost undetectable tinges in her voice that signaled she wasn't completely thrilled with the plan. From the TOS angle, it made sense for my safety and the needs of the organization. It was harder to swallow as someone who wasn't going to get to finish high school or follow through on any of the plans I had for senior year or college.

"Understood," I said in my best, confident agent tone.

Mom cracked and tears fell like I'd never seen from her before. I put my hand on hers and tried to tell her it was okay, but her distress only increased. Dad's hand came down on top of mine, and he also put his arm around her.

"I didn't want this for you. Not ever. Neither of us did." She looked at me and Joanna went to the credenza against the wall and got a Kleenex box. She placed it on the table in front of Mom.

"It's the risk of the job," I said, managing to stay calm—I must've tapped into the same thing that helps her keep focus when I'm upset. "I've known that for as long as I've known what you two do. Yes, this is hard and while I'll miss graduating with my friends, I completely understand why." My voice cracked right at the end.

Lorenzo teared up too. He always looked out for me and periodically expressed concern over how much TOS relied on me while I was so young.

"I knew last night when I said goodbye to Mitch that a part of my life was over. I hadn't expected six months in here, but I get it." I got my composure back, and Mom seemed to find hers again. "If nothing else, in the off hours, maybe Doc and I can have plenty of video game challenges."

"For sure," he said without hesitation, and everyone chuckled as the tension broke.

Mom, Dad, and I kept our close huddle as I continued with a different topic. "Can I ask what's happened with Eddie?"

Mom looked to Joanna in this case. She either didn't know, which wasn't likely, or didn't want to have to break the news.

"Eddie's father has eluded our efforts to apprehend him," Joanna said. "As for what happens going forward, we believe him that he doesn't want anything to do with his father or Blackbird. He also doesn't want to work for us. Certainly he assisted in the rescue of Mitchell Rhodes and, from the debriefing we received from you and D-man, we know he was valuable to you during your captivity."

She took a pause, and I couldn't tell if she was done or not. "In the investigation following the Glenwood case," she continued, her voice strained—clearly not wanting to discuss this with me, "we discovered the point you became compromised. One of the police officers who handled the bike accident was a Blackbird agent who told Cochrane that you'd been nabbed because of your tracker. It was a fault of ours that we didn't have the traffic incident as buttoned up as we thought we did. From there it's clear that Eddie was used by his father and Blackbird."

So the blown cover wasn't my fault after all.

My heart was trying to get ahead of my brain, and I forced myself to take a moment before I spoke. I'd thought this through and they needed to know that.

"What if he comes with me? Starts whatever new life I start? He'll need some sort of security clearance since he'll know I work here but—"

"I don't know—" Mom started.

"What was he supposed to do?" I looked to her, feeling confident in my request. "It's not like he could just go to the police for help." I looked to Joanna. "If I hadn't spoken up, what was the TOS plan for him?"

"We hadn't decided yet," Mom said.

"Okay, so my recommendation is we find something for him to do while I'm here, and then he and I leave together. Maybe we break up before the six months is over, so we'll need a contingency in case that happens. But I want to try to put things back together. I know you can't answer this right now, but think about it. Talk to him and see what he wants. Give him some options. I came into TOS willing, and he's been dragged into all of this."

"I'll think about it and try to leave my 'Mom feelings' on the side."

"We can talk about those as a family." I smiled and got one back from both of them. "But if Eddie wants me back, I'm all in."

Mom wasn't even trying to hide her displeasure, but Dad nodded before stealing a look at his watch. "We have to get to the plane."

"Give me a good funeral, okay?" I grinned at them.

Dad shook his head with a little groan. Who would've thought a funeral could break the tension I'd created. "How can you even joke about that?"

"Might as well. Thinking about it any other way only makes it worse."

"We'll be back tomorrow, and we'll talk. Meanwhile, if something comes up, don't hesitate to call."

"Will do." They got up, and I followed suit as did Lorenzo and Joanna. "Give Mitch and Iris an extra hug, okay?"

"Of course."

We hugged, and they filed out with Joanna. Lorenzo and I hung back.

"Are you holding up as good as you seem?" Lorenzo asked as we stood just inside the room.

I shrugged and threw my hands up. "I think so. It's weird and confusing. But the past couple of days and all the talk as helped."

A small smile broke across his face, but he winced. I shot him a questioning look. "Sometimes it hurts to smile. I'll be glad when that stops. I'm trying to take as little pain medication as I can. Only doing it when my leg gets too fidgety or something. It clouds my thinking too much, and there's no time for that."

"How about I turn the tables? How are you?"

He considered his answer, which I didn't expect. "I have a lot of anger," he finally said, and that surprised me. "This should've never happened. I mean yeah"—he waved his hand in front of his face—"Blackbird could do whatever scheme to disrupt things, but to come after all those people.... And it happened on my watch. I don't want to lose like that again."

I felt the same. I'd vented a lot of anger to Shields.

"To the future," I said as I came up next to him, on the side without the cane, and put my arm around his shoulder. I went for upbeat because neither of us needed to wallow in negativity.

"You sound like Buzz Lightyear." I rolled my eyes and shook my head at him before I released him so he could walk easier as we entered the hall. "Have you seen—"

"Winger?" I turned to the stunned-sounding voice that had interrupted me.

"Oh, wow. D... uhm?" I had my mouth open to speak but didn't know what to call him. I held out my fist, and he greeted it with a bump.

"Locksmith." Dean grinned. "Man, it's good to see you. The news said you were dead. I should've known that wasn't true." He gave a nod to Lorenzo as he came up next to us. "Doctor P, good to see you in person." They did a more traditional handshake.

"You didn't tell me you hired him." I looked to Lorenzo. "That's great."

"I did such a good job working with you, they offered me a gig. I even got to keep my name." He sounded more excited than I'd ever heard him.

"Once Locksmith is done with training, I thought he and Split Screen would make an amazing team."

"For sure," I said, letting Dean's excitement take over. I'd hoped he'd find a place that appreciated his talents. He'd be outstanding here. "We need to catch up once you're settled in."

"Yeah, man."

He stole a look at his watch. "Look, I gotta go or I'm gonna be late for the next session. I'll find you later."

"Cool."

We traded a quick half hug before he took off.

"That's awesome," I said as Lorenzo and I continued toward our offices and the overview of the comm system issues that awaited us.

THIRTY-SEVEN

I stood at Eddie's door shaking.

The first time we met up for a date, I had the same nervous energy. We'd decided on an ice cream place he liked. I'd arrived early, and it gave me time to get super nervous—to the point that one of the other customers asked if I was okay.

I knocked and waited. With no answer, I knocked again, and this time the door opened. After the slightest moment of confusion—maybe I should've told him I planned to stop by—Eddie offered a huge smile.

"Oh my God, it's so good to see you." He stepped forward but then hesitated.

"It's okay, come here." We moved together into an embrace.

"They wouldn't tell me anything about you." His voice was muffled against the side of my head as we continued to embrace.

"I know. It took a while before I heard anything other than you were okay."

"Is the crazy over?"

I shrugged and adjusted so we could look at each other. "I'd say it's a different crazy now."

He nodded slowly, but the smile didn't leave his face. "You want to come in? It's not much, but it's okay."

He stepped aside and lightly took my hand so I'd follow him. The room looked a lot like mine. We both had ragtag furniture—he had a couple of chairs whereas I had a small couch. I liked his desk better—mine looked like a grade school teacher's whereas Eddie's looked like a basic IKEA model that had four legs that screwed into a top. Our TVs and twin beds were identical. He also had a refrigerator and microwave and some basic kitchen stuff like I did. No windows either, which was beginning to make me a little crazy. I made a point to get near a window at least once a day to remind myself what outside looked like.

Eddie looked outside before he closed the door. "No guard?"

I shook my head. "We're done with that. I'm here to talk about what happens next."

"Okay." He drew that out a few extra syllables. "That sounds ominous. Are you here as Winger or Theo?"

"Little bit of both, I guess." I shrugged and brought him over to the chairs. They were set up like a talk show set— both angled toward each other a bit.

I told him about the six-month plan that was in place for me. As I got closer to the rest of the conversation, though, I suddenly doubted if I was the right person to talk about this with him. I had a vested interest in what he'd say. My parents had decided, when it came to who had my heart, it was my choice.

He reached across and grabbed my hand in his.

"Just tell me whatever it is," he said. So much for hiding

my hesitation. "I don't think anything can surprise me ever again."

I squeezed his hand and made sure to look him in the eye. "They want you to stay for at least six months too. Like me, you'd be restricted to this building and any other safe buildings on campus. We're not the only ones that need to live here for a while, so they're working on more comfortable accommodations."

"Okay, so far this doesn't sound too bad."

"We're going to have some minor plastic surgery done to alter our appearances, so we can adopt new identities."

Another nod and even a slight chuckle. "As long as I don't look like one of those people who's had too much surgery, I'm okay with that."

He laughed more, and I joined in. The same thought had crossed my mind when I heard about it.

"I'm told it'll only be what's necessary to fool facial recognition."

He got up and paced across the room, running his hand over his still super short hair. "This is better than the alternatives I've thought up. Let's face it, I wasn't exactly TOS's favorite person. It crossed my mind more than once that they might just eliminate me."

"Well, that's not gonna happen. They want to keep track of you to know where you are and what you're doing. You likely have to check in with someone from time to time."

"So, sort of like probation?"

"I guess." I wasn't really sure that was the way to look at it, but it worked as an analogy.

"What about us?" He looked down to the floor and then at a wall—anywhere but at me. It was cute when his shyness crept out, but this had a tinge of fear too.

"I was going to ask you the same thing." I went to him and gently forced him to look at me.

"Do you...?" The battle raging inside him reflected in his eyes—he forced them back to mine each time they darted away. "Do you want there to be us? Can you even—"

I took his hands in mine and stayed focused on him. "Yes. I want you. I want my boyfriend back. My heart says I can trust you. We're both gonna have to learn how to keep each other safe while I keep the secrets I need to for TOS."

He pulled me in tight, almost making it hard for me to breathe.

"Oh, Theo, I'd hoped we'd get a do-over."

"Me too. No matter how angry and hurt I was, a part of me wanted to work it out."

I craned my head up just in time for his lips to crash into mine. The kiss vibrated through my entire body. We'd kissed on and off since we'd reconnected, but I felt this in my chest and fingers and toes—as if every nerve fired off at once.

I held him tight, which only amped the feelings more. We'd had some crazy good sex before, but it couldn't compare to this kiss. I didn't know feeling this happy and excited was possible. These feels confirmed my heart had given me the right answer about Eddie.

"We should stop," he said while he was still close enough that his lips moved against mine. "I can't lock that door."

"It's okay, my room has a lock. Your new one will too. You'll be moving in the next couple of days."

He nodded and rested his forehead against mine. "Cool." A sigh and shudder moved through him. "What happens if... you know... we don't work out after all?"

"Then we go our separate ways." I used a free hand to

gesture again to the room. "You'll still be connected to the agency, but you won't be forced back to isolation or anything. I made sure of that. You'll get more official details on everything tomorrow."

He nodded and rested his head against mine again.

"I love you, Theo." His brow wrinkled. "Do I even call you Theo anymore?

"For now you can. I have to pick a new name. You'll need one too."

"That's kinda cool, I guess."

"We can figure that out later. How about we go to my place, so we can lock ourselves in?" I asked, and his eyebrows raised. "You don't have to stay here anymore. Your only restriction is to stay in civilian areas."

"Why are we even standing here, then?"

We traded a quick kiss and went to my room for our first foray into being a couple again.

EPILOGUE

NINE MONTHS LATER

I NEVER IMAGINED my life would go in this direction.

Last fall I was starting my senior year of high school. This summer I'm preparing to enter grad school at The University of Texas at Austin.

I'm Maxwell Keller, or Max to my friends. I let my parents pick Maxwell, so I'd still have a name they gave me. Apparently, I was almost Maxwell instead of Theodore anyway. I chose Keller in honor of John, who I missed so much. There's never a day that I don't want to tell him about something or get some advice.

Max still felt pretty new. Three months ago I walked out of TOS HQ with Eddie, and we played the role of a couple new to Austin looking for an apartment. We were supposed to do this in Boston, and it saddened me that Austin had become home. Memories of John, Mitch, Iris, and the rest of my friends could overwhelm me at times. I worked through those feelings with Shields, who encouraged me to try to have a good time finding a place to live.

Eddie and I found a nice, two-bedroom house to rent. With TOS help I converted one of the rooms to a secure office.

I actually enjoyed shopping with Eddie. Somehow one of my least favorite activities became fun as we set up our house.

According to my new identity, I'm nineteen, originally from Des Moines, Iowa where I'd graduated high school early and got my undergrad degree at Iowa State. I'd worked my way through school as a computer tech in campus IT. While I'd actually earned my GED while I'd been cooped up at TOS, I regretted not actually doing undergrad for many reasons. Teaching and research for my masters would be pretty awesome, though.

The most difficult part of becoming Max was the physical transformation. Nearly half a year later, I still startled looking in a mirror. I had a wider nose, a more distinct jawline, and somehow they'd made my eyes wider apart.

Gone, too, was the spiky red hair. It was now jet black and shoulder length. After playing around with a beard last year, I had goatee full-time now. The color change was maintained by a special pill TOS and other agencies had developed to aid in disguises. It modifies the hair color for the entire body. I had to take one every two weeks, or the red would return. My voice had a slightly deeper tone after some adjustment on the vocal cords.

Eddie became Rodney Newell—Rodney was his mother's father, and he wanted to keep something from her side of the family in his name. Newell he picked at random after going through a list of last names he'd googled. He simply liked how they sounded together.

He thought his new face—which the surgeons made overall narrower while also making his nose and eyes somewhat larger—was better than what he'd had. I hated that he felt that way, but apparently he saw too much of his father in himself, and it made him happy that he didn't have to see that anymore. I missed seeing Dad in me, though, and I wasn't sure I'd ever get past that.

We'd spent two weeks in bandages and had them taken off at the same time, facing each other. He smiled at me and, despite the changes, I recognized the wide grin.

"Hi, Mr. Max Keller," he said. "It's good to see all of you again."

"Good to see you too, Mr. Rodney Newell." I smiled right back at him.

The doctor looked at us like we'd lost our minds. We didn't care. As soon as she was done checking us over, we went to my room, ordered pizza, and explored each other to get used to the new look and feel.

Eddie went to the same school. He was now officially twenty and a premed transfer student. Our backstory stated that we'd met at Iowa and came here when I got accepted to grad school.

The six months at Camp TOS, as Eddie called it, had been more difficult for him than me. I had agency work to keep me busy. Even though we ended up with a nice place to live in the TOS building—we'd moved in together about halfway through the six months—he got a little stir crazy. He finally dove into learning how to cook, and we both benefited from that. We discovered our connection to each other still ran deep. We talked a lot—sometimes with Shields—and worked our way back to solid ground.

I was more in love than ever, and the future we'd discussed as regular high school students was mostly back on track.

TOS work kept me busy as I trained new IT staff, worked on security projects and occasionally supported agents in the field. I officially became deputy director of IT security and special projects. That meant grad school might take a while, but that was okay.

I saw Mom and Dad when they were in Austin. They stayed based in DC, with Dad in the field as much as ever. In Mom's capacity as director, she oversaw the missions TOS decided to take and interfaced with the governments that used our services. As planned, Victor and Katherine Reese quietly disappeared, and they got new identities—Ronald and Kimberly Anderson.

A month after my surgery, they were at HQ. While we'd talked routinely and they knew my voice was different, we hadn't had a video conversation because secure video wasn't working as well as we wanted. They met up with Lorenzo and me in the cafeteria, and it was hilarious.

"Doc, it's good to see you," Mom said as she and Dad came up to our table. "You're looking well."

And he was. His bruises had faded and the patch was gone since he had a glass eye—he had a side project to see if he could adapt the contact lenses to work in place of a real eye. The cane was still with him and likely always would be.

"Forgive me," she looked to me. "I don't believe we've met. I'm Director Snowbird."

Lorenzo and I traded looks, and he struggled not to laugh.

I stood and managed to keep a straight face as I came around the table. "Pleasure to meet you, Director Snowbird. I'm Deputy Director of IT Winger."

"Oh my God," Dad said, looking at me with wonder as Mom's mouth dropped open. Lorenzo lost the battle to keep his laughter inside.

Mom hugged me, and Dad came in too.

"It's amazing," she said, lightly touching my face. "If

your parents can't recognize you, that ought to keep you safe."

Shortly after that I decided to put the Winger name to rest too. Theo Reese was gone, and it seemed right that Winger disappear too.

I had Lorenzo to thank for suggesting my new, perfect codename—Netminder.

ACKNOWLEDGMENTS

I'm so thankful for the tremendous team I've worked with on the *Codename: Winger* books.

Dawn was an incredible editor who made the first pass on the manuscripts. I couldn't have asked for a better partner for this series.

Laura provided detailed developmental and structural edits on each of the four books. I won't lie that the first batch of edits she gave me for *Tracker Hacker* had me wondering why I even wrote the book. There were so many notes! But before I was done working through them, I realized she'd made the book tremendously better. After that, I looked forward to her notes. Laura knows Theo, his parents, Eddie and everyone else in the *Winger* universe as well as I do, and I can't thank her enough for her contributions on the series. Truth: a key scene in this book was made a million times more powerful because of her. The suggestions she provided moved me to tears as I read them—that's the kind of impact she's had across this series.

Coming up with a title for this book drove me a little crazy. I have to thank Stacy Agdren and Kate Willoughby for brainstorming with me. *Netminder* is a perfect title, and I don't think I'd have come up with it without their help.

Rachael Herron provided some fact-checking based on her former career, and I thank her so much for the assist.

Will Knauss, my amazing husband, along with Michael Spires, Clint Rebik, Jack Angles, and Julie Angles also helped with this series, and they deserve a stick tap of thanks as the series wraps up.

And while I say *wraps up* here, maybe it's just over for now. I've had so much fun writing Theo that I wouldn't be surprised if you see him and the TOS crew again some day.

YOUNG ADULT BOOKS BY JEFF ADAMS

Each of these titles are available in ebook, paperback and audiobook

Codename: Winger series

Tracker Hacker (includes the bonus short story *A Very Winger Christmas*)

Schooled

Audio Assault

Netminder

Other Young Adult Titles

Flipping for Him

ABOUT THE AUTHOR

Jeff Adams has written stories since he was in middle school and became a published author in 2009 when his first short stories were published. He writes both gay romance and LGBTQ+ young adult fiction...and there's usually a hockey player at the center of the story.

Jeff lives in central California with his husband of more than twenty years, Will. Some of his favorite things include the musicals *Rent* and *[title of show]*, the Detroit Red Wings and Pittsburgh Penguins hockey teams, and the reality TV competition *So You Think You Can Dance*. He, of course, loves to read, but there isn't enough space to list out his favorite books.

Jeff and Will are also podcasters. The *Big Gay Fiction Podcast* is a weekly show devoted to gay romance as well as pop culture. New episodes come out every Monday at BigGayFictionPodcast.com.

Learn more about Jeff, his books and find his social media links at JeffAdamsWrites.com.